IN LOVE WITH HIS WIFE

L.R. JACKSON

Editing By: Julia at Diamond in the Rough Editing

Proofreading By: S. Johnson: Cover Design by James, GoOnWrite.com

Formatting By: Jeff at Indie Formatting

WARNING!

Do not read this book if you are sensitive to abuse of any kind. Scenes from this story can trigger those who may be sensitive to emotional and physical abuse.

For Every Woman who has Survived and in memory of those who didn't!

NOTE FROM THE AUTHOR

Unlike my others, this story was not easy to write. Nor was it as fun to write. I probably won't market this book like I do my other ones because it's not meant for that purpose. I didn't write it for the sales. I wrote it for ME. Although this is a love story, I had to tap deep into my past to create these characters. It was an emotional roller coaster for me. I stopped writing it a few times and almost shelved it for good. I didn't think I could do it, but I did, only I made it a novella to protect my mental sanity. Tristan's character drained me—he brought back memories I try to forget. So, the story you're holding in your hands is all I could give. I hope you understand.

I AM A DOMESTIC ABUSE SURVIVOR!

Whew, I've never said those words out loud. Only those close to me know what I've gone through. This is not a true and factual story about my life. It's loosely based on my experience with physical, mental, and emotional abuse. This story won't be for everyone, which is why I added a disclaimer in the beginning.

But I needed to write it. For me and for the many other women who suffer from abuse.

There are many misconceptions surrounding domestic abuse. Most think the solution is easy, they say "you should just leave." This is why most women remain silent. Because of their fear of judgment. Most do want to leave. They don't stick around because they enjoy it. But it can be harder to get out than you think. IF they make it out at all. There are some difficult scenes in this story, but there are also some pretty dope ones. There are times you will be angry. Times you may cry. But I promise you a happy ending.

If you decide to stick around and read it, THANK YOU!!!!
Xoxo
L.R. Jackson

IN LOVE WITH HIS WIFE

My life was in perfect order.

I had my career as CEO of a fashion empire, a beautiful fiancée, and more money than I could spend in two lifetimes.

But that was before I met *her*.

Zara Price.

One look into her beautiful brown eyes and I was hooked. I was ready to burn my whole life, every careful plan I'd ever made, to the *ground* if it meant I could have her.

The problem is...she's married.

And her husband just happens to be my best friend from college.

He doesn't deserve her, though. He's neglected and mistreated her, broken what I'd gladly devote my life to cherishing. So, I'm starting to not even *care* that she belongs to him.

The fact is, there's no *me* without *her*. Not anymore.

Soon, she'll have to make a choice. And in the end, she *will* choose me.

I'll make sure of it...one way or the other...

CHAPTER 1

ZARA

My makeup case falls to the floor, and I bend down to pick it up quickly, hoping I don't wake Tristan. I have an interview today, and I've been excited about it all week. If they hire me, it'll be just what I need to gain some work experience. I've tried endlessly to get my foot in the door in the fashion industry, but with waitress jobs plastered across my resume, it's been impossible. I open the makeup case and look at myself in the mirror, crossing my fingers that I can cover up my black eye. I have the routine down to a science now. Thanks to my raging husband, I've become a pro at covering up my bruises. I make my makeup look flawless, and when I leave the house, I add the icing on the cake...oversized sunglasses.

But today is different. I won't be able to wear sunglasses during an interview. I won't be able to avert my eyes and turn my face the other way. I'll need to remain attentive. Be transparent. And that's hard to do when someone's staring at you, wondering who punched you in the face. Tristan walks inside the bathroom. "What the hell is that noise? I'm trying to sleep."

"Sorry, I didn't mean to wake you. I dropped my makeup case." I apply my foundation and avoid eye contact with him.

He lifts the toilet seat. "You never *mean* to do anything, do you?"

I stay silent because it's the only way I can guarantee that this conversation doesn't get out of hand and I end up with two black eyes instead of one. I work the makeup brush, paying close attention around my bruise, while he pees. When he's done, I hear the toilet flush, along with the sound of the toilet seat slamming down.

Please go back to bed. Please go back to bed.

He doesn't. He walks over to the double sink and turns the water on to wash his hands. "Where the fuck are you going this early anyway?"

"Remember I have that job interview today?"

"Oh. Yeah, it's about time you pull your weight around here."

I nod. But not with agreement. I nod as an acknowledgment of his statement. Pull *my* weight? I do more than my fair share around here. I might not have a job right now, but I cook all his meals. Keep his clothes clean. Keep the house clean. And entertain his boring-ass colleagues when they come over. He dries his hands then hugs me from behind. "You know, Zara, last night wouldn't have happened if you'd watched that mouth of yours. No wife of mine is going to talk back to me. I'm the man of the house. Which means I own it and everything in it, including you."

Talk back? All I said was that I didn't feel up to having a beer at two in the morning.

His green eyes meet mine through the mirror. He's started phase one. The scolding. Followed by the speech about how I've been a bad wife and I deserved what was coming to me. "I'm sorry, Zar." There's phase two. The apology. That always comes directly after the scolding.

Fuck you, Tristan. You're always sorry.

"I mean it this time. It won't happen again."

He waits for my response. "Okay." I grab the lipstick in front of me and smile at him before I put it on. If I don't show him the attention he *thinks* he deserves, he'll become angry. He watches me for a few minutes before he lets me go. "Don't be out too long."

"I'm coming home as soon as the interview ends."

"Good. Don't forget an old friend of mine is in town. We're meeting him for dinner."

"I didn't forget. I already ironed your clothes."

He leans in and speaks firmly in my ear. "Don't embarrass me tonight."

I smile nervously. "I won't."

He chuckles. Takes a step back and smacks my backside. "You bet your sweet ass you won't."

I arrive to the interview twenty minutes early. My leg bounces up and down with nervousness as I wait to meet the head designer for Minnie's Boutique. It's a small boutique located in Atlanta, but it's ahead of the game with designs. All the celebrities and well-to-do people shop here. My eyes dart between the pieces of clothing on display. They're gorgeous. Trendy. I would even consider them high-end fashion. But they're not better than mine. I've had a love for fashion since I was a kid. I used to play around in my mother's closet, arranging outfits for her. She would scold me for sneaking into her room and going through her things. But then I would see her wearing the very same outfit I picked out for her. I was never the popular girl in school. Or the smartest. I did well enough to pass. But my grades were often neglected because I kept my head down in my

3

journal, sketching pieces of clothing. I couldn't wait to graduate high school and chase my dream of becoming a designer. My family had other plans though, and I never made it to designer school. Well, not after graduation anyway.

The receptionist calls my name. I stand to my feet and follow her down the hall. We arrive at a conference room, and she opens the door for me. "Mrs. Lewis will be with you shortly," she says as she closes the door.

I place my briefcase down, take a seat, and tap my foot lightly as I wait. I hate doing these. I must have interviewed over fifty times by now, yet still no job. I need to be as impression-able as possible today. Because I need this. I can't hear the word *no* again. The door opens and in walks a tall, striking woman. "Mrs. Price. I'm sorry to keep you waiting."

I stand, extend my hand, and shake hers firmly. "No problem at all. Thank you for meeting with me today."

She gestures for me to take my seat, and once we're seated, she scans my resume. "You graduated from Atlanta's Elite School of Design."

There was nothing Elite about it. Mediocre professors who know nothing about real fashion.

"Yes, I graduated top of my class."

"Hmm, and no work experience yet?"

"Not yet. But designing comes naturally for me. I've been sketching since I was a kid. As a matter of fact, I brought some of my designs for you to review."

She doesn't respond and continues reading my resume. "Is there any reason why you decided to wait to attend design school? Most people start right after graduation. Looks like you waited a while to enroll and complete your studies."

Yes. There are multiple reasons why. Reasons I can't explain to you.

"I had some personal issues that affected my ability to enroll. But I assure you—"

"I'm sorry, Mrs. Price, but we're looking for experienced designers. I'll give you a call if an entry level position opens."

But I need this job.

I nod. "Thank you for your time."

I allow the bubble bath to release some of the stress I'm feeling. Another rejection. So, what if I haven't had the chance to work in the fashion industry yet? I'm better than most of the designers out there. And I could prove it if somebody gave me a fucking chance. I didn't think it would be this hard. I didn't think it would take me this long to find a job. I have no money, other than the spending money Tristan gives me every week. It's just enough to cover my hygiene products, groceries, and art supplies. Without my own income, I have no way out. I didn't plan on being in this situation. This isn't the life I wanted. I had dreams. And I planned to follow those dreams. But my parents didn't support them. When I told them about what I wanted to do, my mother was disappointed, and my father was furious. He spent years trying to convince me to work for his company, but I wasn't interested. My father owns a defense technology firm. It's made him millions. I grew up wealthy. Privileged. But I didn't care. I didn't participate in after school activities. I didn't hang out with friends. I locked myself in my room and sketched. My mom thought I would grow out of it, and my father thought something was mentally wrong with me. I told them that I wanted to be a designer, but he demanded I attend college and receive a degree in business or politics. I didn't want to do it, but I did it anyway. Because my father had a way of forcing me to do things.

I enrolled at Atlanta University and met Tristan my sophomore year. We met in my economics class and hit it off. He was charming and handsome. Living on a college campus wasn't a good fit for me, but he had a tiny apartment just around the corner from the main building. I spent a lot of time at his place. Mainly because I hated being home. I hated the pressure from my father. And I hated the naivety of my mother. She saw what he was doing. She knew it bothered me. But she said nothing. She did nothing. As always. Why? Because my father and Tristan share something in common. They're both controlling. Emotionally abusive. Evil. She feared the consequences of standing up to him, and quite frankly, so did I.

After two years of college, I realized I was miserable. I couldn't do it anymore. I couldn't tolerate sitting through another course that wasn't related to design. So, I dropped out. And my father gave me an ultimatum. Either I finish school, or he would cut me off financially and kick me out. I refused to go back. I didn't care what the consequences were. So, I gathered some things and moved in with Tristan permanently. He had a job and offered to help me save money and attend design school. Things were great at first. I worked odd waitressing jobs, saved a little money, and purchased myself a car. Tristan graduated with a degree in politics and got offered a position on a political campaign. After four years of dating, he proposed, and we got married right away.

Tristan later ran for mayor and won. And I became the wife of a political figure. Image became everything to him. He made it clear that we had standards to uphold. The mayor's wife couldn't be seen serving burgers at the local Burger Spot. I could only work if I took a job that made us look good as a couple. So, I quit my waitress job and became a housewife. I didn't mind at first. But then things started to change. Tristan started working longer hours. He became moody. Withdrawn. Little arguments turned into bigger arguments. Those bigger arguments turned physical. I wanted to run home after the first time he hit me. But my father was no better than him. Running home would have been the same as moving across the street in Hell. So, I stayed. Choosing one evil over the other.

TYSON

"Have you seen my tie?"

"I put it on the bed," Charlie yells from the bathroom.

I reach the bed and grab my tie. I'm meeting Tristan in an hour, and I'm still not ready. Charlie walks out of the bathroom and stands beside me as I place the tie around my collar. I turn my head to face her. "What?"

"We're going to be late. Why can't you ever be on time?"

"I'm almost done." I secure the knot and spin around. "There. See?"

She places her hand on her hip and frowns. "Well?"

"Well, what?"

"Aren't you going to say something about my dress? It's a new one."

"Charlie, every dress you wear is new."

She crosses her arms and stays planted in place, waiting for a compliment. "Sorry, honey. You look beautiful."

Her frown turns into a smile. "Thank you. I'll wait for you downstairs."

I shake my head as I watch her sashay out of the bedroom. What the hell was I thinking by asking her to marry me? I'm the creator and owner of the fashion empire Tyson Wear. It's a line of high-end ties, cufflinks, and shirts. I met Charlie at a fashion show in New York City about a year ago. When I met her, I had just hit the Forbes list. I had it all. The money. The reputation. The status. But something was missing. A wife and kids. I wanted the complete package. A successful career and a woman who compliments me. Someone who is beautiful, humble, and caring. Charlie is *not* that woman. Well, maybe except for the beautiful part. She's one of the most beautiful women I've ever laid eyes on. And I've seen some beautiful women in my lifetime. But she's self-absorbed. Selfish. She's high maintenance and narcissistic. I have no one to blame but myself. Because I knew all of this when I asked her to marry me. I chose to settle for her instead of giving myself time to find the right woman.

Charlie never complains about how much I travel. She doesn't care that my job takes priority over our relationship. Enjoying the perks of being engaged to Tyson Reed is what makes her happy. I got comfortable being with a woman who allowed me to be married to my career. I get away with a lot of shit because of who I am. I don't have to give my *all* to her. She doesn't care about my past, my dreams, or anything outside of what my bottom line is. I'm able to solely focus on work without the distraction of planning date nights, remembering anniversaries, and rushing home before dinner. She's every CEO's dream, and I thought this was exactly the kind of woman I should be with. But as time passed, I realized that I craved more. I desired a woman who would hold me accountable if I came home too late. A woman who asks me how my day was. Someone who shares the same interests as me. Someone who desires *all* of me. Someone who cares. I tried to draw myself closer to Charlie the past year, but she made it clear that she's happy with things exactly as they are. The only thing she's concerned about is pulling off the wedding of the century.

I hate to sound like I'm bashing her because I'm not. She has some great qualities. She's fun. Spontaneous. And knows the ins and outs of being with a man like me. She knows what to say when we mingle with executives. She knows how to charm my competitors. And she looks good on my arm doing it. But that's where our compatibility ends. I wish I could say I love her. But I don't. And I doubt I ever will. So many times, I wanted to tell her the truth. That I rushed into proposing. I wanted to tell her that she deserves to be with someone who loves her unconditionally, but that man isn't me.

I grab my wallet and take one last look at myself in the mirror. I'm excited to finally catch up with Tristan. Tristan and

I both worked at a pizza shop near the campus of Atlanta University. He needed the extra money to cover college expenses, and I needed to help my mother pay her bills. We were best friends his freshman year. I lived vicariously through him, attending college parties, sleeping with every girl I could get my hands on, and drinking like a fish. We vowed to keep the party going. I was even going to try to enroll into school myself. But then my mother died. I became depressed and quit the pizza shop. I packed my things and moved to New York City with my aunt. Tristan tried to stay in touch, but I was in no mood to talk to him or be reminded of how things used to be.

I grab my suit jacket and head downstairs. Charlie is standing by the fireplace waiting for me. She's wearing a white wrap dress that accents her honey-coated skin. The black heels make her five-foot-three frame seem taller. And her hair is styled perfectly in a bun. She's beautiful. She flashes her pearly whites when she sees me. "Don't you look dapper."

"Thank you."

She loops her arm through mine. "We look good together, Tyson. And once we're married, we're going to make one hell of a team."

Married. There's that word again. Every time she says it, it makes me sick to my stomach. It doesn't feel right. I need to tell her, but it'll have to wait until after dinner.

We arrive at the restaurant right on time, and I hand the valet the keys to my Mercedes. We enter the building and are met by the hostess. I give her our name, and she leads us back to the table where Tristan is already seated. He stands to his feet. "Tyson fucking Reed."

He moves around the table and pulls me in for a brief man

hug. I take a step back and look at him. "I can't believe it. It's been a long time, Tristan."

"Yeah, well, I tried to stay in touch, but it was almost impossible now that you're a big shot. Thank God for social media."

"You got lucky. My assistant runs my Twitter account. She took your direct message seriously and asked me if I knew who you were."

He laughs out loud. "I knew it. I knew there was no way in hell you would be posting those sappy-ass inspirational quotes."

Charlie interrupts us by clearing her throat. "I'm sorry. Tristan, this is my fiancée, Charlie."

He extends his hand to her. "Wow, man, she's beautiful."

"At least somebody notices," she responds.

"It's nice to meet you. Are you from Atlanta as well?"

I don't hear her answer. And I no longer hear Tristan's voice. The world stops around me, and my eyes are fixed on the woman walking toward us. She's breathtaking. The emerald dress she's wearing fits snug, like it was painted on her. The split climbs up her cinnamon-colored thigh. Her shoulder-length hair bounces as she walks. It's like she's gliding on air. She stops when she reaches Tristan's side. He and Charlie end their conversation. "Tyson, this is my wife, Zara."

She takes a step closer and places her dainty hand inside of mine. It's soft and velvety. "It's a pleasure to meet you."

"Likewise."

Her voice is husky. Sexy. I zero in on her light brown eyes, and that's when I notice it. She's tried to cover it up with makeup, but she can't fool me. I've seen those same bruises on my mother's face. My eyes swing to Tristan after I pull my hand from hers. He wouldn't. Would he? Could this be the same guy who was my best friend all those years ago? Maybe I'm overreacting. Maybe her bruise was caused by something else.

Charlie interrupts my thoughts. "I'm Charlie. Tyson's fiancée."

I blink my eyes rapidly to bring me back to focus. "Shall we have a seat?"

I pull the chair out for Charlie. When she takes her seat, I notice that Tristan has seated without pulling Zara's chair out. I walk around the table and pull it out for her. "Tristan. Don't tell me you've forgotten how to be a gentleman."

He chuckles. "Was I ever a gentleman?"

Zara thanks me in a voice so low, it's almost a whisper. Once I sit down, I try to scan the menu, but my eyes discreetly move to hers. She lifts them to meet mine but lowers her gaze when the waitress arrives. After we've given our order, I take the risk and get a good look at her face. Yup, definitely a black eye. Anger shoots through me. Who the fuck would hurt a woman so goddamn beautiful?

"So, you're in Atlanta for good?"

"Yeah, just opened my office here six months ago."

"Completely different from New York, I imagine."

"Yeah. But New York was good to me. I can't complain."

"Well, there's no place like home. I'm glad you're back and we're able to reconnect."

"Yeah. It feels good to be back. How about you? Are you taking care of the great city of Atlanta?"

"Hell yeah. Between you and me, I'm about to run for governor. You're the first to know."

Zara's face fills with surprise, but not in a good way. "I don't doubt you at all, Tristan. You've got my support."

It's a lie. Because my support for him depends solely on if he's hitting his wife. He smiles before he turns his attention to Charlie. "What about you, Charlie? What do you do?"

"I'm a celebrity makeup artist," she boasts.

"That's very interesting," he replies.

Curiosity gets the best of me. "What do you do for a living, Zara?"

"Zara doesn't work," Tristan answers for her.

She looks embarrassed but remains quiet. "Tristan, I'm sure she can answer for herself."

Her eyes land on mine. "I haven't been able to find work," she answers softly.

Charlie interjects. "Did you go to college?"

"Yes, briefly. I graduated from Atlanta's Elite School of Design."

No fucking way!

"You're a designer?" I ask almost too excitingly.

"Well, not officially. But I'd like to become one."

Tristan huffs. "She likes to draw. I hardly call that design."

It's confirmed. The guy I thought I knew, the guy I used to be best friends with, is a complete asshole. And I suddenly don't want to be around him, let alone admit that I even know him. Zara looks uncomfortable. "Do you have a portfolio?"

Her eyes shine brightly at my question. "Yes. And I made the dress I'm wearing."

You mean the one I want to peel off you right now?

"Tristan, why didn't you tell me your wife graduated from design school?"

"I didn't think it was important."

"Nonsense. And I'm always willing to help a friend. Zara, I've been looking for an assistant. Why don't you stop by my office and we can work out the details?"

"I thought you hired one already," Charlie chimes in.

I did. But she'll be fired as soon as I send an email.

"She was incompetent, so I let her go."

"I..." She pauses for a second and looks over at Tristan, waiting for him to approve.

She's scared of him. I've seen that look in my mother's eyes plenty of times before. Tristan frowns. "Thanks, Tyson. But Zara can find something on her own. She just needs to give up this fantasy of becoming a designer and get a *real* job"

My blood is boiling. I want to reach across the table and

choke him to death. This is not the guy I once knew. "I'm sure she's capable of finding her own job. But I'm offering the chance to work directly with me. Not many people get this opportunity, Tristan."

He's quiet as he thinks. Probably looking for other reasons to turn me down. Zara speaks to me softly. "That's awfully nice of you. I'd love to be considered for the job."

Tristan glares at her. His eyes tell her that she's made a mistake by speaking up. And that she'll pay for that mistake later. I can't believe I agreed to meet an abuser for dinner. This arrogant bastard has no clue how much I despise men who disrespect or hit women. There's so much I want to say. So many ways I want to suggest she leave him. But if I've learned anything at all, it's that an abused woman will only leave her abuser when she's ready. Push too hard, and she'll resist. She barely knows me. She won't listen to me. Even if I tell her how much I understand what she's going through. So, I must do this. I need to hire her. Have her close so I can keep an eye on her. Tristan finally agrees. "I guess it'll be okay."

I pull out my business card and hand it to her. "Great. Come by tomorrow morning around nine."

I had completely forgotten that Charlie was sitting beside me until she speaks. "Don't let him intimidate you either, Zara. He can be tough when interviewing candidates."

I won't be interviewing her. The job is hers.

Her fingers brush mine as she takes the business card from me. She places it inside her purse and smiles. "Thank you."

"You're welcome. You're married to Tristan, so that makes us family now, right?"

He answers for her. "Yeah. Thanks a lot, man."

I can tell by his tone that he doesn't mean it. He's pissed that I offered her a job. Pissed that she'll be working right beside me. He shakes it off and resumes the conversation. As the night continues, Zara and I steal glances at each other. She's quiet most of the time as the rest of us engage in conversation. Charlie picks Tristan's ear about life as a mayor. He speaks with excitement as he explains it to her. But me, I don't care about what either of them have to say. Because there's only one thing I'm interested in learning about. And she's sitting right in front of me.

CHAPTER 2

ZARA

"What the fuck do you think you were doing back there, Zar?"

"I was only being nice to your friend, Tristan. You said I needed to find a job, right?"

"I meant a job that didn't involve working for my friend."

"I thought you would be happy."

He drives erratically. Weaving in and out of traffic and running stoplights. He's scaring me. I grab the handle to the doorknob tightly with one hand and hold on to my seatbelt with the other. "Happy? Why would I be happy about the fact that you made me look like a fool? You made a decision without me."

Beads of sweat drip from his forehead, and his fingers grip the steering wheel tightly. He shakes his head. "You *know* I don't like you working alone with men."

I keep quiet. It's what I do when he's this angry. Anything I say might trigger him more. I know he doesn't like me working alone with men. But I thought Tyson would be safe. After all, they are friends. I can't believe Tristan is friends with *the* Tyson

Reed. Billionaire. Voted sexiest man alive. Fashion genius. Visions of him flood my brain. As I exited the ladies' room, he was the first person I saw. He's a hard man to miss. My eyes did a quick sweep of his attire, and everything about what he wore spoke money. Power. I have a keen eye when it comes to high-end labels. One look and I knew exactly what he was wearing. He was dressed in an Armani suit and a pair of Salvatore Ferragamo loafers. Even his tie was expensive. He looked rich. Successful. I felt like the wind got knocked out of me as I got closer to him. His brown eyes held mine. Captivating me. When I took my place next to Tristan, I was able to notice his neatly trimmed beard and smooth milk-chocolate skin. My insides tingled as he shook my hand.

He watched me throughout dinner, although he tried not to make it obvious. I know because I also stole glances of him. I watched the way his luscious lips wrapped around the straw when he sipped his drink. I watched how his forehead wrinkled whenever his phone buzzed with an incoming message. I watched the way his chest rose and fell with each breath he took. I loved watching him laugh at Tristan's jokes. I loved hearing him speak. His baritone voice soothed my unsettled anxiety. His fiancée is a lucky woman. I take a deep breath at how low I've sunken.

Really, Zara, lusting over your husband's friend?

"Do you hear me talking to you?"

Tristan's voice brings me back to focus. "I'm sorry. What?"

"I said, you call him tomorrow and tell him you can't accept the job."

My heart sinks. "But Tristan, it's a good opportunity for me. For us. I'll be able to contribute more."

"You're not taking it. We don't need a handout. Get your ass out there and find a job on your own like the rest of us."

I turn and face the window. I knew he would try to take this from me. I've been interviewing for months now, and I'm finally offered a job. And not just any job. A job with Tyson Reed. CEO of Tyson Wear. This would be a huge opportunity for me. My big chance.

We arrive home, and Tristan slam's the front door behind us. He follows me upstairs and spins me around roughly when we reach the bedroom. "You made me look weak, Zar." His nostrils flare with anger, and his fists ball at his sides. Just as he raises a hand at me, his phone rings. He pauses mid-air. "I'll deal with you later."

He walks away and answers it, and I look up to the ceiling with relief. "Thank you, God," I whisper.

Most nights are rough. But some nights are easy. Those are the nights I'm grateful for. The nights I thank God for. I'm not overly religious, but I've spent so many nights praying through the punches. The kicks. Asking for them to stop. Asking that the next strike doesn't hurt more than the last. If I can spend all that time begging God for his help, I'd like to think that I have an obligation to at least thank him for the nights I'm spared. Tristan walks out of the walk-in closet. He's changed into a pair of jeans, a T-shirt, and a pair of sneakers. "I'm going out for a while. Don't wait up." He brushes past me and out the room.

I release the breath I'm holding when I hear the front door slam. Don't wait up? I never do. Tristan often comes home late. Those are my favorite nights. The nights I get to spend alone. I sleep safe and sound until he ruins it by climbing into bed, apologizing for being out late and reeking of alcohol. As if I care. I don't care how late he gets in. I barely like the sight of him, let alone lying next to him. Most of the time, I hope he doesn't come home at all.

I head downstairs to the dining room and grab a bottle of wine from the wine rack. I select red tonight. I pop the cork, grab a glass, and head back upstairs. I place the bottle and the glass on the nightstand. I change quickly into a pair of black tights and a white T-shirt, then I tie my hair into a bun and grab my supplies out of the closet. One day, I hope to have my own space to sketch and sew. Every time I found a room to work in, Tristan needed it for something. After a while, the empty rooms became occupied with his campaign stuff and I was left with only a tiny space in our closet. I keep my supplies in a corner and sew at the dining room table. I pour myself a glass of wine and stretch my legs out on the bed. I prop a pillow behind my back and start to sketch the dress that's been occupying my mind for weeks now. Dresses are my favorite to create. I love how sexy a dress can make a woman feel, no matter how insecure she is on the inside. My eyes focus on the outlines and shading as my image starts to come to life. Designing is my outlet. It's something that's embedded in every fiber of my being. I may be jobless. Broke. And stuck in an abusive marriage. But this, this is my gift. And no one can take this away from me.

My eyes pop open, and I look at the clock. Seven a.m. I release the black-colored pencil still in my hand and shove my sketchbook to the side. I turn over and look at Tristan's side of the bed. He's not there. Good. Because I don't feel like hearing him badger me about turning down this job today. I'm supposed to call Tyson and decline his offer. But that's unprofessional in my opinion. I owe it to him to tell him in person. Besides, Tristan isn't here, so it's the perfect time for me to get out of the house for a few hours. I brush my teeth, shower, and get dressed. I grab my purse and briefcase, make sure I have his business card, and head downstairs. I pause as I pass by the living room. Tristan is passed out on the couch, fully clothed and reeking of vodka. I tiptoe past him slowly. I don't want to wake him. He'll ask me where I'm going and forbid me to leave the house once I tell him. I reach the front door, open it carefully, and sprint to my car as fast as I can.

After sitting in traffic, I finally arrive at Tyson's office, and it's everything I thought it would be. Enlarged magazine covers sit on every wall. Each one showcases a new design. Photos from his various fashion shows occupy the available white space. My eyes swing to the fabric samples enclosed inside of frames and plastered on the tables in the waiting area. "Mrs. Price, he's ready for you."

I follow the woman down the hall. Her tight skirt enhances the hips that she sways from side to side. She opens the door to a conference room when a voice sounds from behind us. "Not in there, Pam."

I turn around and almost lose my balance. Tyson deserves the title of sexiest man alive. I've never seen anyone who could take my breath away, until now. His sky-blue button-up outlines his broad shoulders and sculpted arms. A pink tie sits snug around his neck. The slacks he's wearing are perfectly tailored and stop right before the black loafers on his feet. Pam swings her blonde hair to the side. "Are you sure, Mr. Reed? We always place your candidates in the conference room."

He stops directly in front of us. "She's not a candidate. She's my new assistant. I've got it from here."

I want to tell him that's not the case. That I came here to turn down his offer. But I don't feel comfortable telling him in front of her. She spins on her heels and leaves us alone. Tyson smiles. "Zara, let's talk in my office."

We arrive at his office, and he closes the door behind us. My eyes go wide at what's in front of me. Huge, wide glass windows allow perfect light to fill the space. His long wooden desk sits at an angle where he has the perfect view of the Atlanta skyline. The drapes are a canary yellow and match the canary-yellow rugs I'm standing on. Decors of reds, yellows, and grays are spread through the room. A red chaise sits in the corner, and

L.R. JACKSON

the room smells like fresh apples. He walks over to his phone and presses a button. "Pam, please hold my calls."

"Sure, Mr. Reed."

He turns to face me. "Have a seat."

He gestures at the plush gray chairs placed in front of his desk. His eyes shift down as I cross my legs. Is he checking me out? No. He couldn't be. I'm his friend's wife. And he's engaged. "Did you bring your portfolio?"

"Yes. I have it right here, but Mr. Reed…"

"Call me Tyson," he demands.

"Mr. Reed. I came here to tell you in person that I can't accept the job. I was wondering if you could maybe write me a letter of recommendation for someplace else once you've looked at my work."

He raises a brow. "Someplace else?"

My mouth parts to answer, but nothing comes out. I'm afraid I've offended him. He extends his hand. "Let me take a look."

I hand him my portfolio. He takes a seat on the edge of the desk as he flips it open. He studies my work intensely while I sit quietly, nervous about what he could be thinking. Does he like my work? Does he think I'm an amateur? Finally, he flips it shut and watches me for a few seconds. "I haven't seen talent like this in a long time, Zara."

My heart beats rapidly. "You like it?"

"Like it? You are what this industry needs right now. These designs, they're refreshing, edgy, unique."

My mouth curves wide as I burst with excitement. Tyson Reed likes my work. I knew my work was good. But hearing it from him gives me the extra boost of confidence I didn't know I needed. "Thank you. You have no idea how much it means to hear that."

He crosses his arms. "You belong in fashion, Zara, and I can help you get there. Now, tell me, why is it you can't take this job?"

TYSON

I'm starting to think it was a mistake to ask Zara to work for me. The minute I saw her, I wanted to lock us both in my office and show her how it feels to be treated by a *real* man. There's no way I can work closely with her if she dresses like that every day. The red pencil skirt hugs her curves and showcases her tiny waist. The black blouse under her red suit jacket shows just enough cleavage. Her hair hangs loose around her shoulders, and those heels...dammit, those heels. I wonder what she would look like naked and wearing only those. The scent of her perfume drifts past me as I wait for her to answer my question. I already know the answer. But I need to hear her say it. Her eyes cast down. "I...I just can't."

I want to lift her head up. Show her that she should never lower her head in the presence of any man. *Anyone* for that matter. "Is this about Tristan?"

Her head jerks up, but she doesn't answer me. Instead, her eyes search mine, wondering what I know. I continue. "Tristan won't be a problem."

She shakes her head. "What do you mean?"

"We met for drinks last night and talked it out. His only stipulation is that I don't show you favoritism. That you get the same treatment as all my other employees."

As if that will happen. I can already tell she's special, and I'm going to treat her that way.

She still looks puzzled. "And he's okay with me working with you?"

"Yes."

She's at a loss for words. She's waging a war in her mind. She's relieved and happy. But also worried and confused. I decide to pry further. "Zara, is there some other reason why he wouldn't want you working with me?"

Her eyes hold mine, and I try to push the anger I'm building deep down inside. Every time I look at her face, I see red. Every time I see that bruise, it reminds me of what Tristan does to her behind closed doors. She blinks a few times before she answers. "No. He just worries about us accepting handouts, that's all."

I smile. "Don't be concerned about that. I may have agreed to help you, but this..."—I point to her portfolio—"your work speaks for itself, Zara."

"Thank you, Mr. Reed."

I stand to my feet. "I'll buzz Pam to bring your new hire paperwork. Can you start today?"

She nods. "Yes."

It only took Pam a few minutes to bring the paperwork I asked for. But it's taking Zara some time to sign it. I watch her as she scans the papers in front of her. She's been reading it for over twenty minutes now, and I'm starting to think she's changed her mind about working for me. "Is everything okay with the terms?"

She looks up. "Yes. Everything looks in order."

Then sign it.

She looks down at it again, then looks back up at me. "I was wondering about one particular section."

"Which one?"

"The schedule. It says I'm available outside normal business hours."

I lean back in my chair. "I'm extremely busy, Zara. I work around the clock; therefore, I need my assistant to be available around the clock as well."

She nods. "I understand. But..."

"What is it?"

"Tristan often has work functions. He often makes public appearances. He likes me by his side when he does. I'll need that time off, and I'll also need a few hours free in the evenings to make sure dinner is done before he gets home."

You've got to be kidding me.

He doesn't deserve her. He hits her. Belittles her. She gets the job she's been dying for and yet still finds time to think about his needs. Assholes like him always end up with the good ones. I nod. "I can be flexible. Whatever you need."

Her body relaxes. "Great." She finally signs the damn thing and hands it to me. "Thank you for the opportunity, Mr. Reed."

"Tyson."

"Do your other employees call you Tyson?"

"No. But they're not my assistant. You are."

"I see."

I place the papers down on my desk and stand. "Follow me."

When I open the door, I gesture for her to walk in first. She takes a step inside and looks around. "What is this?"

"This is your adjoining office."

She smiles. "Wow, it looks brand new."

That's because it is. She has no idea of the lengths I went through to get this office looking good. Once I offered Zara the job, I texted a friend of mine who's a contractor. I asked him to spruce up the office. Make it nicer. He thought I was kidding, asking him to work on an office space at night. But he found out just how serious I was when I offered him triple of what he would make if it were a regular day job. Thank goodness he already had the supplies on hand. He added fresh paint, lush blue carpeting, and an adjoining door. I wanted her office to be as nice as possible. She sniffs. "It smells like fresh paint."

"I had maintenance add a fresh coat. I wanted to spruce it up a little. These offices can get rather old, you know."

She spins around. "This is a state-of-the-art building. I doubt you needed to do much."

I walk over to her desk. "Nope, not much at all. I hope you like it."

She smiles. "It doesn't take much to make me happy. I would have been happy working in a closet if it meant I'd get to work for you."

Somehow, I sensed that. That it's the simple things that matter to her. I get the impression that she's humble. I smirk. "Is that so?"

She blushes. "I mean…it's just…it's an honor to work for you, Mr. Reed."

"You mean work *with* me. And please, call me Tyson." She blushes again. "It's an honor to work with someone as talented as you, Zara. I can't wait to see all the things you can do."

I'm so close to adding the words *to me* at the end of that sentence, but that wouldn't be professional. And it wouldn't be right. She's married. To Tristan. And even though he's an asshole, we have history. And that makes her forbidden. I take a step forward and feel something hard under my foot. I lift my leg. It's a nail. I bend down, pick it up, and make a mental note to call my head of housekeeping. They were supposed to have this place spick and span before I got here this morning. I even paid them overtime to come in earlier than their shift. What if Zara had stepped on this and twisted her ankle or something?

Why are you so protective of her?

I hold the nail tightly. "Sorry about that, I guess housekeeping missed this."

She shrugs. "I'm sure it was a simple oversight."

I should fire the whole team and hire a new one.

"Right."

She takes a seat in her new plush leather chair. "This is soft. And comfortable."

"Good. Because you'll be in it a lot."

"Are you in your office a lot?"

"No."

Her eyes swing to mine. "Oh."

"With my meetings and traveling, I don't get to spend much time in my office."

But I'm about to change that.

"I understand."

An expression crosses her face. An expression I don't like. She looks uncertain. Nervous. And she shouldn't be. She's going to have no problem doing this job. "But I'll be with you every step of the way until you're ready to work independently."

Relief washes over her. "Thank you, Mr. Reed."

"Tyson."

She smiles again before she turns away and starts her computer. When her name pops up on the screen, I give her the login credentials and allow her settings to appear. "Looks like you're all set. I'm going to step away and let you complete those pain-in-the-ass new hire courses. Let me know when you're done."

"Okay. Thanks."

She clicks on the first online training course titled *Sexual Harassment in the Workplace.* I straighten my tie, turn around, and close the door behind me.

CHAPTER 3

A few hours later, she walks through the door. "I'm all done."

I look up from my cell phone. She's taken her suit jacket off, and I get an even better view of her cleavage. Lord help me. "Okay. Have a seat. There are a few things I'd like to go over with you."

She takes a seat in front of my desk, with a pen and pad in hand, eager to take notes. Eager to learn. For some reason it turns me on. The sight of her in that tight skirt and fuck-me heels sitting in front of me just as excited about the fashion world as I am makes me so fucking hard, I can barely concentrate. I shift in my seat. "Your laptop and iPhone should arrive this afternoon."

"What will I need those for?"

"Remember. I'll need you accessible."

"Except for the times we agreed upon, right?"

I smile. "Right."

She nods her head in acknowledgment. "Good. Let's get started."

It's around lunchtime when we decide to take a break. I've shown Zara how to access my email, my schedule, my client list, and the accounting system. Once we finished with the basics, I showed her what I knew she wanted to see the most. The fashion design software. Her face lit up like a Christmas tree. She was amazed as I explained the Tyson Wear design process from A-Z. She was able to see a design from a rough sketch all the way to its completed stage. Her eyes shined brightly as she watched the screen. She absorbed every single syllable that left my mouth. I know that look. She lives for this. This is her passion. She would get so excited that she would lean over me to look at my computer screen. It was torture having her that close to me and not be able to touch her. I shake away those thoughts. What the fuck is wrong with me? I shouldn't be having those thoughts. When she cocks her head to the side to write something down, I see that bruise again. And I become furious all over. Is this why I've developed a mini obsession with her? Am I trying to save her? The way that I couldn't save....

The sound of my phone buzzing interrupts my thoughts. "Mr. Reed, your lunch is here."

We take a seat at my conference table, and I pass her a salad. "I asked Pam to order from the deli from across the street."

"Is she your assistant too?"

"No. She's the office receptionist."

"Oh."

"I hope you like chicken Caesar salads."

"One of my favorites. Thank you."

I take the opportunity to ask her some questions while she's chewing. "Are you originally from Atlanta?"

"Yup. Born and raised."

"And you've always wanted to be a designer?"

"Yes. Since I was a kid. I went to college and studied business for a few semesters before I dropped out."

"Why did you drop out?"

"I never wanted to go to college. I only went to please my

father. Once I saw how miserable I was, I couldn't do it anymore. I had to do what I knew would make me happy."

How can a woman so sure of what she wants stay with a man who mistreats her?

"Good for you, for pursuing your dream. Not everyone has the courage to do that."

"I never thought I would have the chance to do what I love, but here I am."

We take sips of our waters. "How did you meet Tristan?"

"At Atlanta University. We're college sweethearts."

"Really? I used to visit him on campus. I don't remember seeing you two together."

"We met his sophomore year."

"Ah, yeah, I had left for New York by then."

"Why?"

"Let's just say I needed a change."

"I see."

She turns the tables on me. "How did you meet Charlie?"

"At a fashion show."

"I should have known. She looks like a model."

I chuckle. "She wasn't one of the models. She was there to do their makeup."

"Are you excited about the wedding?"

There won't be a wedding if I can help it.

We're interrupted by Pam. "Mr. Reed. Charlie is on line two for you."

"Excuse me for a minute."

I walk over to my desk and pick up the phone. "Hey."

"I thought you said you would call me after your morning meeting so we can discuss the wedding."

"Sorry, I got pretty busy here with Zara's first day and all."

"I can't believe you hired her. She doesn't even have experience."

"What do you need, Charlie?"

"I found a venue. I think we should do an early June wedding, before it gets too hot. What do you think?"

"Sounds good. Can we talk about it later? I've got Zara in my office right now."

She's quiet. "I don't like you working so closely with her, Tyson."

My eyes flick over to Zara, who's checking her own cell phone. "Why not?"

"I just don't."

"You have nothing to worry about, okay?"

"Promise?"

I cross my fingers behind my back. "Promise."

"Okay. Can I at least show you the pictures of the venue tonight?"

"Yeah."

"Okay. Bye."

We end the call, and I take my seat across from Zara. "I'm sorry about the interruption."

"I understand. She's your fiancée. She's important."

I don't confirm or deny her statement. "So, tell me, what do you like designing the most?"

"Dresses."

"Why?"

She thinks for a second. "There's nothing more dangerous than a woman in a sexy dress."

I smirk as visions of the dress she wore last night enter my brain. "You're right about that."

CHAPTER 4

ZARA

I had a short first day. Tyson got dragged into some conference call and decided we would resume tomorrow morning. As I pull into my driveway, I realize my glimpse of a perfect day has ended. Tristan will be home from work soon, shifting my mood from happy to irritated. I open the front door and kick my pumps off. I walk upstairs, change into a pair of sweats, and rush to get dinner started. If I don't have dinner ready as soon as he walks through the door, it really sets him off. I whip up some meatloaf, place it in the oven, and decide to wash a few loads of clothes while it cooks. After it's done, I prepare some roasted potatoes and some sautéed broccoli. I glance at the clock. Ten minutes before he gets here. Just in time. Luckily, I won't have to deal with this too much longer. I re-did my plan today, and by my calculations, I'll be able to leave Tristan sooner than I originally planned. Tyson is paying me very well. I'll save enough money, get my own place, and divorce Tristan. Just as I take a beer out the refrigerator, the doorbell rings. I swing the door open. "Tyson."

He hands me a box. "Your laptop and phone."

"Come in."

He enters, and I close the door behind him. We walk inside the kitchen, and I place the box on top of the table. "Thank you for bringing them by."

"You're welcome."

I find a pair of scissors and start to open the box, but he softly grabs my hand. "Here, let me."

I release the scissors to him, and he cuts through the cardboard with ease. He removes the Mac computer and the iPhone and hands them to me. I glance at the clock. Tristan will be here any minute, and I don't want him to walk in on this. "Would you mind if I take these upstairs?"

He shakes his head. "Sure."

I hurry upstairs with the phone and laptop and place them inside my briefcase. I hurry back downstairs, where Tyson has already thrown the box in the trash. He smiles. "It smells good in here."

"I'm making meatloaf."

I don't look my best right now. My sweats have a grease stain on them, and my tank top has breadcrumbs stuck to it. My hair is twisted unruly in a ponytail. I really wish he had called before dropping by. "Can I get you something to drink?"

"Sure."

I walk over to the refrigerator. "Water, tea, soda?"

"Tea would be good."

I pour him a glass of tea and hand it to him. "So, how was the conference call?"

"Stressful."

"How so?"

"One of my shipments was bad."

"What do you mean?"

"The thread that I use for the buttons on my shirts is top of the line. It's called power thread because of its strength and durability. One of the features of my shirts is a one-hundred-percent guarantee that the buttons will never pop, loosen, or frazzle. Well, the company that makes the thread was taken over by a new owner. That owner decided to cut corners and tried to send us phony thread."

I gasp. "How did you find out?"

"I do a thorough inspection of all my materials. Well, not me personally, but my team does."

I look apologetic. "So, what happens now?"

He cocks his head to the side. "I don't know. What do you think should happen?"

"You want *my* opinion?"

"Yeah. I do."

"Fire the supplier but only after you've made them recuperate your loss of income. Then sue them for breach of contract.

He smirks. "I like the way you think."

TYSON

She's smart. Smarter than what Tristan gives her credit for. And she looks stunning right now. Tight-fitting sweats, a tight tank top, and bared feet, showcasing neatly manicured toenails. I'm fighting the urge to pick her up, carry her upstairs, and fuck her on the bed she shares with Tristan. I'm going to hell for these crazy thoughts. And as bad as it sounds, I'd be willing to take the trip if I could just have one kiss with Zara.

"How did you know where I live?"

"From your paperwork."

"Oh, yeah. Stupid question, huh?"

"No. Nothing you ask could ever be stupid."

The sound of the front door slamming alerts us that Tristan is home. "Zara, where are you? I've been calling you all fucking day."

She immediately stiffens. I want to defend her, but I can't." Tristan walks into the kitchen and halts when he sees me. "Tyson, what are you doing here?"

"I dropped by to give Zara a few items she'll need for work."

He glances between us before heading to the refrigerator. "How was her first day? Did she fuck anything up?"

He laughs as he pulls out a beer, but I don't see anything funny. There's nothing amusing about disrespecting your wife. I want to put him in his place. Badly. But if I do, he'll force Zara to quit. Then I won't be able to keep an eye on her. And I need to keep an eye on her. I need to make sure she doesn't end up like...I bury the memory of *her* back where it belongs. "She's exactly what I need. I'm glad I hired her."

Tristan takes a sip of his beer. "Well, at least she's finally doing something productive with her life."

Zara looks uncomfortable as Tristan belittles her. He looks her up and down. "What the hell are you wearing, Zar?"

She looks down at her clothing. "Sweats. I just finished dinner."

"We have company. Can you change into something presentable?"

I can't do this. I see the tears forming in her eyes. I'm so angry I want to explode. My body tenses. My fingers flex. My pulse speeds up at the sight of her tears. "That's not necessary. I shouldn't have dropped by unannounced. I'll see myself out."

"Wait, won't you stay for a beer or two?"

You want me to share a beer with you after what you just did? Hell no.

"Thanks, Tristan. But I need to get home. I promised Charlie I'd be home in time for dinner."

He chuckles. "If I had a fine fiancée like her, I'd rush home too."

I speak in a low and firm voice, trying my hardest to control the beast fighting to be unleashed. "Tristan. Your wife is standing right here."

He looks over at Zara as he chugs a swig of beer. Once he swallows it, he laughs out loud. "I'm just fucking with you, Tyson. Zara knows how I am. Don't you, Zar?"

She nods and he continues. "Come on, since when did you get so sensitive?"

My eyes meet hers. "I'm not sensitive, Tristan. I'm respectful. And you of all people should know that."

"Yeah, yeah. Let me grab another beer, and I'll walk you out."

When he turns his back to open the refrigerator, I mouth the word *sorry* to Zara. I feel horrible about what just happened. I should have never stopped by unannounced. Because I did, it gave Tristan the opportunity to belittle her in front of me. She offers a subtle headshake. Silently telling me it isn't my fault. I hold her stare until I'm forced to turn away when the refrigerator door slams. "Are you sure you can't stay?"

I smile at Tristan. "Thanks, man. But maybe some other time. Zara, I'll see you tomorrow."

She smiles as she lifts her hand and waves goodbye. Tristan walks me to the door, and a feeling of unease creeps through me. I don't know what he could do to her once I leave. He could hurt her. But I can't do shit about it. I step outside of the house, feeling defeated. "Thanks for stopping by, Tyson. See you soon."

I seriously doubt he means that, but I go along with it anyway. Because I have no other choice in the matter. "Yeah. See you soon."

ZARA

As soon as Tristan walked Tyson to the door, I ran upstairs and powered on my new iPhone. My instincts told me I would find something important on it. And I did. Tyson's client list is already programmed. My email is set up, and my calendar. But those aren't what's important. What's important is the message already waiting for me from him.

Tyson: Zara, call me if you need anything. No matter the time.

I place the phone back in my briefcase. How embarrassing I felt just now. Standing there, powerless, while Tristan berated me in front of Tyson. I was humiliated. That's not the version of me I wanted Tyson to see. He can't see me weak. Destroyed. Broken. He needs to see that I'm strong, resilient, fearless. That's the kind of woman who deserves to work by his side. That's the kind of woman he'll be able to trust with his business. But Tristan ruined it for me. And Tyson is probably thinking he hired the wrong person for the job. Tristan enters the room. "What did he bring you that was so important?"

I shrug. "Oh, just a computer and phone I'll need for work."

He leans against the dresser. "You think you're better than me now that you got a fancy job?"

"What? No. I'm an assistant, Tristan. That's it. There's nothing fancy about it."

Fancy isn't the word to describe working with Tyson. Its life changing. But I need to downplay it to Tristan. He's quiet for a minute before he speaks. "We'll, I've decided to let you keep the job. You can at least pay some bills around here."

"Thank you."

Gratification. Tristan feeds off it. He loves when he thinks he's allowed me to do something. He's in for a rude awakening when he comes home one day to find me gone. Forever. He walks toward me. "You know, you actually look attractive right now."

He pushes me back on the bed and climbs on top of me, kissing my neck. I hate when he wants to have sex. I hate the way he feels. The way he breathes. The way he smells. It's not that I don't find him attractive. His caramel-colored skin, green eyes, and perfect physique make him the perfect eye candy. It's the mean words that repulse me. The physical attacks that keep me at a distance. The way I've been treated over the years has stripped away everything I ever felt for him. The thought of him on top of me naked, breathing heavily in my ear as he fucks me like a prostitute, makes me want to vomit. I try to get out of it. "Tristan, I'm tired."

He stops kissing me. "Are you rejecting me?"

The rage in his eyes is instant, and I regret saying anything. "No, I..."

He grits his teeth. "Then. What."

"I just had a long day."

He climbs off me and stands beside the bed. "Oh, I get it. You get a job now and forget who you belong to?"

I climb off the bed and try to reason with him. "Tristan, I..."

The punch to my face happens so fast I don't have a chance to shield myself from it. I taste the blood forming in my mouth right as the pain starts to settle in. "Shit, see what you made me do?" He points a finger at me. "You better remember your place. The sooner you do, the better things will be for you."

He rushes out of the room. When I hear the front door slam, I hurry to the bathroom to assess the damage. My top lip is bruised and swollen. I turn the faucet on and spit the blood out in the sink. I take a warm cloth and wipe the blood from my lip and teeth before heading downstairs to grab an ice pack out of the freezer. It's one of many that I keep for this reason alone. I bring it upstairs with me, lie across the bed, and place it on my lip.

I should kill him for what he does to me. Maybe cyanide. Boric acid. Something to make him die in his sleep.

I quickly erase those thoughts. As much as I wish he could pay, I'm not a killer. If I just stick to my plan, I can be out of here soon. Warm and happy thoughts fill my brain as I think about the endless possibilities of being free of Tristan. I'll have my independence back. My self-worth. I'll sleep peacefully knowing I won't be woken up by yelling and screaming or damn near being raped in my sleep. I place the ice pack down and do what I always do when I need to clear my mind. I sketch. I scatter my materials out in front of me when I hear a beep. I walk toward the noise and find it coming from my briefcase. It's my work phone. I pull it out. There's a message from Tyson.

Tyson: I'm sorry I stopped by unannounced. I should have called first.

Me: You have nothing to be sorry for.

Tyson: Is everything okay? Tristan isn't angry with you, is he?"

Yes, he's angry. So angry that he punched me in the face.

Me: Everything is fine.

Tyson: I meant what I said, Zara. Call me if you need anything. And I do mean ANYTHING.

What does he mean by that? Does he know something? Does he know what type of man Tristan really is? I shake my head. Maybe I'm reading too much into it. I don't respond to his text. I delete the text, power the phone off, and place it back in my briefcase.

CHAPTER 5

TYSON

I've been on edge all night, pacing the floor in my man cave. Zara hasn't responded to my last message. Maybe I was too intrusive. I hated leaving her there, alone with Tristan. I know that sounds stupid because she's his wife. They live together. Of course, she would be there alone with him. But my gut feeling told me something was off. It told me he would hurt her the minute I pulled out of the driveway. I plop down on my couch and place my head in my hands. This is not my business. This is their life. If she wants to stay with a man who treats her horribly, then who am I to convince her otherwise? Women who are abused never listen to the people who care about them anyway. They ask for your help. Cry on your shoulder. And when you tell them to leave, they do the exact opposite. They go back to him. They make excuses for why they do it. And it's the same cycle all over again. That's why it's best not to try to help. It's best to stay out of it. I've been down this road before. I should know better.

It wasn't easy convincing Tristan to allow Zara to work for

me. I invited him out for drinks after we all had dinner together. I could tell he was angry at Zara for wanting to take the job, so I wanted to get him out of the house for a while to cool off. We met at a bar and had a few rounds of shots. He was wasted after round one. He bragged about his career. His money. How Zara answers his every beck and call. I sipped my glass of cognac and tried not to smash it against his skull. He's an idiot, and it saddens me. I was looking forward to reconnecting with him. Catching up with an old friend I once respected. But now, I wish I never agreed to have dinner with him. I should have left our friendship in the past. Right now, I'm no longer interested in rekindling it. I'm only interested in helping Zara get in a position where she can leave him. Something my mother never got the chance to do.

"Are you coming to bed?"

Charlie folds her arms across the skimpy white nightgown she's wearing. "I'll be up in a second."

"Tyson, you've been down here for hours. You promised we could look at the wedding venue tonight."

"I know. Just give me a few more minutes."

She takes a deep breath. "Just forget about it."

She stomps away, and I gulp the rest of my drink, intending to do just that. Forget about it.

I arrive at work early the next morning just in case Zara needs help with anything before I get dragged into meetings. The adjacent door is open, and her light is on. I place my briefcase down and approach the door quietly. I knock softly. "Can I come in?"

"Yeah, come in. I'm just trying to connect my phone charger. The USB port is in a weird spot."

I walk inside to find her bent over her desk with a cord in her hand. She's wearing a purple sleeveless dress with her ass on full display. I watch her from behind. Jesus, she's going to be the destruction of me. "Let me help you with that."

She turns around to hand it to me, and I freeze. "What happened to your face?"

Her lip trembles slightly. "Oh, um, I accidently tripped over a pair of shoes. Damn heels are everywhere."

Her laugh sounds forced, and her voice is shaky. She's lying. I'm sure my blood pressure is through the roof right now as anger courses through every vein in my body. Images of Tristan striking her make my ears pound and my throat go dry. I connect the cord and gesture for her to sit down. She takes her seat. "Zara, I know I just met you. And I'm your boss. But please understand that you can talk to me. In confidence."

She allows my statement to settle in before she answers me. "I'm okay. Really."

Coming to work with bruises on her face tells me that she's far from okay. But she works for me. I can't pressure her to tell me the truth. It wouldn't be professional, and it's disrespectful to press her about her personal life. "Okay."

She smiles, trying her best to hide how she's really feeling. "So, what are we doing today?"

"Today, we're working on items for my next fashion show."

She grins wide. "That sounds exciting."

I nod in agreement and remain calm. Even though I want to punch a wall right now. "It is. Come on, I'll show you what we have so far."

ZARA

There was something about the way Tyson watched me just now. There was something about the way his jaw clenched right before he asked me about my face. Does he know I lied about what happened? It doesn't matter. Even if he *thinks* he knows, he can't prove it. I'm seated on his couch, with pen and paper in hand. He's quiet as he fiddles with the remote for the huge monitor mounted on the wall. An image finally pops up on the screen, and he takes his own seat. He's on the opposite end of the couch, yet I can still smell his cologne. I can also feel the tension rolling off his body. Is he angry with me? I take a deep breath. Of course, he would be angry. He just hired an assistant who comes to work with bruises on her face. How would that go over with his clients? Other members of his staff? Shit! I need to do something about this. I can't lose this job. Maybe I'll talk to Tristan about it. I quickly decide against it. Tristan won't care. If anything, he'll find humor in the fact that he's left his mark on me. "These are the items for my new line."

Tyson's voice returns my focus to the screen. I smile at what I'm seeing. Sexy men. In suits of all colors. "Wow, they look amazing."

My eyes are glued to the screen. Drinking in every detail. Every feature of the suit and how it does or does not compliment the man wearing it. "Thank you. These are just a few samples. If they're well received at the fashion show, we'll go full scale with them."

"In every color?"

I can feel his eyes on me. "Yes. Why do you ask?"

I turn to face him. "Well, Tyson Wear is known for luxury items made from the finest materials and crafted by experts best in the business, right?"

He throws his arm across the back of the chair and smirks. "Right. Go on."

"Your items are purchased by men who exude power. Wealthy men who buy nothing but the best no matter the cost. Just last year, your revenue increased by seventy-five percent when you started to sew your ties by hand."

"What are you saying, Zara?"

"Think about the men who pay top dollar for your designs. Your target market is CEOs, well-to-do businessmen, celebrities, people who don't care about dropping over three hundred dollars on a tie."

"And?"

I point to the suit on the screen. "Do you honestly think any of the people I just mentioned would buy a lime green suit? Would *you* wear a lime green suit to a meeting?"

He rubs his chin as he thinks for a second. Then he looks at me and chuckles. "No. I guess I wouldn't."

His eyes swing to the screen in front of us. "My marketing director thought it would be good for my brand. She thought it would be nice to step outside of the box."

"It is a good idea. Times have changed. Colors are getting bolder. Brighter. Offering different colors could boost your sales, but you have to be smart about it."

"What would you recommend?"

"I think you should start with the basics. Colors wealthy men have been wearing for years. Black. Blue. Gray. Feature those in your fashion show, let it be known that Tyson Wear now offers suits for the *CEO In You.*"

"The *CEO In You*, I like that."

I smile. "Once your suits are offered in every store, I think we should do limited editions to roll out the different colors. Maybe one or two at a time. Whether or not that color will be offered permanently will be based off those sales."

He pauses the screen and stands to his feet. He walks back and forth a few times, deeply in thought. He stops in front of me. "It's a brilliant idea."

I release the breath I'm holding. "Really?"

He takes a seat on the edge of his desk and folds his arms. "Come here, please."

I place the pen and pad down and stand. I cross the room and stop in front of him. He uncrosses his arms and looks me straight in the eyes. "One thing you need to know about me is that I don't say things I don't mean. I told you it's a brilliant idea because it is."

I nod, and he continues to speak. "Be confident in your work, Zara. Be confident in your ideas. Be confident in *yourself.*"

"I understand. I'm sorry if I..."

He cuts me off. "Stop apologizing. You've done nothing wrong."

"Okay."

His eyes stare into mine. The way he's looking at me causes me to grow hot. It causes my stomach to flip-flop. He stands upright, and swallows thickly. My heart pounds as he takes a step toward me. He's close to me now. So close, I can feel the heat of his breath. Is he going to kiss me? Please let him kiss me. He places his hand under my chin. My lips part, hoping he gets the hint that I want his mouth on mine. And I want it badly. He tilts my head back. He leans in. And I close my eyes.

"Mr. Reed. Charlie is here to see you."

The voice startles me, and I jump back. Tyson narrows his eyes before he walks around his desk and presses a button on his phone. "Send her in."

"I'll go to my office."

He stops me. "Zara."

"Yes?"

"I'm sorry. I crossed the line and I..."

Before he can finish, Charlie bursts into his office. "This is the second time in a row you've forgotten to call me."

"I'm sorry. Zara and I were just wrapping up."

Charlie watches me with suspicion. "Zara. It's nice to see you again."

"You too, Charlie."

"How are you liking the job so far? My Tyson can be demanding. Isn't that right, sweetheart?"

I hold my head high. "I'm making out well. Thanks for asking."

The energy shifts in the room, and it's not a positive shift. Charlie hates that I'm working with Tyson. I can feel it. "Well,

I'll leave you two alone. Tyson, I'll be in my office if you need me."

TYSON

It's a good thing Pam's voice came across the speaker. Because I was about to kiss Zara. And if she had let me kiss her, I'm sure it would have ended with me fucking her on top of my desk. Cliché, I know. Fucking your assistant in your office. But with Zara, it wouldn't be about the sex. Yeah, she's sexy as hell. With curves that'll leave any man drooling. But it's her energy that I'm attracted to. She's like a bright light at the end of a tunnel. A breath of fresh air. She's smart. Opinionated. And the sad part about all of that is, she's only like that when she's here at work. There are two versions of Zara. When she's here, she can be herself. When she's home, I know she's being whoever Tristan wants her to be. I get glimpses of that part of her when she second-guesses herself. When a loud noise makes her flinch. When she lowers her gaze as if she isn't worthy. I notice it all. And I hate what he's turned her into. "What are you thinking about?"

Charlie interrupts my thoughts. "The fashion show."

"Work as always. You're so dedicated to your career, Tyson. It's what I love most about you."

"This is a busy time for me, you know that."

"I know. But I have the best news."

"What is it?"

"I found us the perfect castle in Paris."

"Castle? Paris? As in, Paris, France?"

"Yeah. You said we could have an extended honeymoon there."

"Charlie, I don't remember having that conversation."

"I asked you last month. Remember, we were lying in bed? It was right before you did that thing that I like."

That explains a lot.

Charlie chooses the most inopportune times to ask me for something. Right before we have sex is one of them. It usually results with me uttering a bunch of uh-huhs, yesses, and whatever you want. Now, it's backfired on me. Had I really been listening to what she was asking, I would have told her no. "Charlie, I can't leave Atlanta right now. Not with everything going on with the fashion show and the launch of my new suit line."

"So, when can you leave Atlanta?"

"I don't know. But we have plenty of time to have the wedding and honeymoon."

She folds her arms across her chest. "I don't understand you, Tyson. You ask me to marry you but refuse to set a wedding date. And every time I try to discuss the wedding, you're too busy."

She's raising her voice. And the last thing I want is for any of my staff to hear. Or Zara. "Can we talk about this later?"

"No. We need to talk about it now. I don't ask for much of your time, but this is important. So, what's the holdup?"

"There is no holdup, Charlie. What's the rush?"

"Our engagement is the biggest news of the year. People are expecting an outlandish wedding. My friends and family are all asking me when the date is. And I have nothing to give them."

"Are you marrying them or me? We don't set a wedding date based on when the world wants us to, Charlie. We set a wedding date when it's convenient for us."

She takes a step forward. "Six months. I told you I wanted this wedding to happen in six months."

"I know. But with this new line and taking Zara under my wing..."

"Zara? Are you seriously telling me that you don't have time to plan a wedding because you're training your friend's wife?"

"No. That's not what I'm saying. Charlie, please, can we discuss this tonight?"

Her eyes glance at the door behind me. "Really, Tyson, an adjoining office?"

"Since when are you this insecure?"

"I'm not insecure. I'm territorial. I see the way she watches you."

"That's ridiculous."

She shifts her Saint Laurent bag to the other shoulder. "Whatever." She pauses for a second, "I'll see you at home."

CHAPTER 6

ZARA

I spent the rest of the afternoon typing up a to-do list of things we needed to finish for a successful fashion show. When I went to my office, I kept myself busy, trying not to eavesdrop on their conversation. I could hear their raised voices. She didn't sound happy, and neither did he. When his door slammed shut, I didn't see him for the rest of the day. I'm about to grab my briefcase when he knocks on my door. "Glad I caught you."

"Come in."

He steps inside. "Zara. My actions earlier were unacceptable. I promise you it won't happen again."

"It's okay. I wasn't exactly innocent."

"I take pride in being professional. I don't know what came over me."

Probably the same thing that came over me.

"Let's just forget it happened."

Although I won't.

"Okay."

"Tomorrow, I have a meeting with the designers and our marketing team. I'd like you to join."

"Yes, of course."

"Could you do a presentation for the team? Show them what we discussed today?"

"Sure. No problem."

"Okay, then. The meeting is nine a.m. in the conference room."

"I'll be there."

"Have a good night, Zara."

I watch him leave my office. Regretful that I didn't get to feel his lips on mine. It's sinful to think about kissing my husband's friend. It's downright ugly of me to want a man who belongs to someone else. But I can't help it. Tyson sees me. He sees the woman I really am. He's kind. He's respectful. And he believes in my work. He took a chance on me when no one else would. Which is why we can't cross the line. The last thing I want is to become the designer who slept her way to the top. I have too much respect for him, myself, and his brand. But...a woman can dream, right?

I'm doing the dishes while Tristan scrolls through his phone. "Dinner was delicious, baby."

I turn around and smile. "Thank you."

He walks over to me and wraps his arms around me from behind. "How was work?"

Careful how you answer him.

"It's work. It pays the bills, right?"

He chuckles. "Right. How much is Tyson paying you anyway?"

Lie.

"I'm starting at a beginner's salary. Forty thousand a year."

That leaves me with twenty thousand dollars that he'll never know about.

"That's it?"

"Yeah, for now. I may get a raise at the end of the year."

"Tyson's decent. He'll reward you if you work hard."

"Good to know."

He spins me around. "I want to talk to you about something."

"Okay."

His eyes scan my face. They land on my lip. "Zara, I'm not proud of the things I've done to you."

I don't respond.

"I promise to do better. I don't know what comes over me. I just...lose it sometimes."

I still don't respond.

"I'll try my best to be more patient with you. I know you're still learning how to be a wife, and it isn't easy. I need to give you time to grow into the woman I know you can be for me. For us."

I nod. "Thank you."

He kisses me on the lips. "I'll see you upstairs."

He's on the phone when I walk into our bedroom. He glances at me and lowers his voice while he talks. Could he be talking to another woman? My hopes remain high as I slide into a pair of pajamas and slide into bed. If Tristan is seeing someone else, that puts me at an advantage. Maybe he'll spend more time with her. I doubt he'll leave me any time soon. Not with him entering his bid for governor. He'll need arm candy. The image of a supportive, beautiful wife. I close my eyes, pretending to be asleep when he ends his call. I feel the bed dip beside me, and he exhales loudly. His arm wraps around me, and he strokes my breast. I don't want this. I don't want him touching me. But I know better than to resist. He leans in and kisses me on my neck before he turns and lies on his back. I breathe deeply with relief. "I don't get excited to fuck you either." I breathe softly and evenly. "I know you're not asleep, Zara."

"I was almost asleep."

I can feel him turn and look at me in the dark. "You're lying. I felt you tense as soon as I touched you."

Does he think I can possibly *want* to have sex with him with the way he treats me? He continues to speak. "Zara. I work my ass off to take care of us. Is it too much to ask for you to do your job as my wife?"

I do everything he asks of me, and he knows it. But I play along. "I'll try harder."

"Don't try. Do."

"Okay."

I think the conversation is over, but he grabs my face tightly and turns it around to face him. He squeezes it so hard that I think he'll break my teeth. "You know what my expectations are. Now, I said I would try to be more patient with you, and I will. But that doesn't mean there won't be consequences. Do you understand?"

I nod. "Zar, do you understand?"

"Yes," I answer in a muffled voice.

He releases my face. "Good. Good night."

A tear slides down my face. "Good night."

I'm up early the next morning and out the house before Tristan wakes. I wake up with a purpose now. A reason to keep going. A plan for a better life. I place my briefcase down and log on to my computer. I already have an email from Tyson requesting me to double-check the proposed venue for the fashion show. He wants to debut his line in two weeks, so that doesn't leave us much time. I Google the name of the establishment and start to do my research. About twenty minutes pass before there's a knock at my door. I turn around to face Tyson. "Good morning."

"Good morning. I was just writing down my notes about the venue."

He walks inside my office. "Did you find an issue with it?"

"Actually, I found a few."

He approaches my desk. "What did you find?"

"Well, the first issue is parking. This venue is in the city. People will need to pay the meter or pay to park in a garage. If they're already buying a ticket to the show, the least we can do is choose a place where there's free parking."

"They're rich, Zara. Paying for parking is a drop in the bucket for them."

"That may be true, but it's the principle."

He's quiet for a second. "What's the other issue?"

"The parking garages are blocks away, which means people will have to walk in the heat, ruining their best clothes by sweating. Not to mention women in heels. Definitely a no-go."

He chuckles. "Anything else?"

"Yes. For the money you're spending, Wi-Fi should be included. But they offer it as a separate package."

"Hmmm, all good points. Doesn't sound like this place is a good fit. Do you think you could find us a better one?"

I smile. "I already had a place in mind."

He smiles back, but then his smile turns into a frown. He searches my face before he shoves his hands inside his pockets. "Another accident?"

"What?"

"Your face. You have a bruise on your cheek."

Tristan's grip left marks on my face. I tried my best to cover them up this morning, but I guess I failed. "I told you. I'm clumsy."

He's quiet for a second. "Zara, is someone hurting you?"

I shake my head. "No. What makes you think that?"

He points to my face. "The bruised lip. The black eye you tried to cover up. They don't look like accidents to me."

I debate if I should be honest with him. He would be the first person I've told. I feel safe when I'm in the office. I feel safe when I'm around Tyson. But I quickly conclude that I can't tell him. He's Tristan's friend. His loyalty is to him. "Really, Mr. Reed, it's nothing."

"It's nothing? If you're being hurt, it's everything."

He knows. And no amount of makeup or excuses can hide the truth from him. My eyes become teary as I become fearful. Fearful about losing my job. I'm working for one of the top designers in the world. I was supposed to impress him. I was supposed to make him happy about his decision to hire me. But instead, I've dragged my personal life into the workplace. "Are you going to fire me?"

He scrunches his face. "Is that what you're worried about?"

I nod.

He takes a deep breath. "Zara. I'm not going to fire you. That's something you don't have to worry about while working for me. But I am concerned."

"I'm sorry. I promise I won't bring my personal life into the workplace again. I'll figure something out."

He shakes his head. "You're not hearing me. I'm not concerned about you doing your job. I'm concerned about *you*."

His eyes meet mine and before I can stop it. The tear falls. Shit! Day two on the job, and I'm crying in front of my boss. I wipe my tears with the back of my hand as I struggle to get it together. Tyson reaches for a tissue and hands it to me. I grab it, and our fingers touch. I look up at him, hoping I don't see eyes of pity. When his eyes lock onto mine, it's not pity I see. It's anger.

CHAPTER 7

TYSON

As soon as that first tear fell, I was doomed. Pure and violent rage blasts through me as I watch Zara wipe her tears. I want to console her. Hug her. But I promised myself that I would remain professional from here on out. "Zara, I..."

She stands and interrupts me. "I'm okay."

"It doesn't look like you're okay. I want to help you."

"You're Tristan's friend."

"We were close once. But I'm not sure if I could call us close friends now."

She shakes her head. "There's nothing you can do. Let's just move on."

"But—"

"Tyson, please. Just forget about it. I'm here to do my job, that's it."

I don't want to forget about it. I want to take her down to the police station, make her press charges, and hire her the best divorce attorney there is. But I also know that I can't *make* her do anything. She has to want to do it on her own. I can't fight her on this. If I do, it'll push her away, just like it did with my mother. I hand her another tissue and smile. "I finally got you to call me Tyson."

This makes her laugh. She dries her tears and smiles back at me. "Thank you."

"If you ever need my help, just know that you can come to me."

She nods. "Okay, but can we get back to work?"

My mind has been occupied all evening. It got so bad, I agreed to go over the wedding list with Charlie, just as a distraction. I keep wondering if Zara's safe. If he's hurting her right now. I shouldn't be thinking about her so much. I shouldn't be worrying about another man's wife. But from what I can see, that's part of the problem. She doesn't have anyone to worry about her. Where are her parents? Friends? "That's not a good match."

Charlies voice interrupts my thoughts. "Huh?"

"My sister cannot sit next to your uncle Jimmy. He'll flirt with her all night like he did with me last Christmas."

"She's single, so what's the problem?"

She playfully punches me. "Tyson! The problem is that he's sixty years old and she's thirty-one."

"Hey, they say age is just a number. Everybody needs love, right?"

She places the notebook down and straddles me. "Right. And I'm so happy I found the love of my life."

She places kisses on my neck as she unbuttons my shirt. Once my shirt is opened, she kisses my chest, then kisses her way down until she's on her knees. I take a swig of the cognac I'm drinking as she slides her hand inside of my custom-made Tyson Wear pajama pants. I should be hard as steel right now.

My dick should be throbbing at the thought of being inside her mouth. But it's not. My dick is not hard, and I'm not turned on. I lift myself up as she slides my pants down. I take another gulp, hoping it helps light the much-needed fire in my groin. She wraps her lips around me. It does nothing. I throw my head back and close my eyes, trying to concentrate. She swirls her tongue around the tip and stops. "What's wrong?"

"Long day," I reply without looking down at her.

She stands. "Work's never interfered before."

I place my glass on the end table and slide my pants back up. "I'm sorry, honey. My mind has been occupied with this fashion show. How about I make it up to you later?"

She plops down beside me. "Deal. Let's get back to the wedding list. I think five hundred people should be the max."

"Five hundred people? Charlie, I don't know five hundred people."

"Sure, you do. Your business associates. Models. Celebrity friends."

I shake my head. "I do business with those people. A wedding should be *close* friends and family."

"True. But it's also going to be a big event. *People Magazine* offered to feature us. Tyson, we have to invite the right people."

I shove to my feet. "I'm not paying for a wedding to show off. The day is about us. Not anyone else."

"You're a billionaire. Do you honestly care about how much we spend? It's our wedding. We should be able to splurge as much as we want."

I stand up. I can't do this with her. Not right now. Not while I'm already going crazy worrying over Zara. "Let's talk about it later."

She follows me to the bottom of the steps. "We are not putting this off again, Tyson."

I spin around to face her. "Fine. Invite whoever you want."

I walk up the steps, eager to get some space from her. This

is getting out of hand. I've got to let her know that we're making a mistake by getting married. And I've got to tell her soon. Before she sends out five hundred invites. I remove my phone and pull up the name that's been burning in my brain all night. My fingers hover over her number. Debating if I should reach out to her. I say to hell with it and type a message.

Me: I need to know that you're okay."

I place the phone on top of my nightstand and open the second drawer. I pull the photo out and brush my finger across her face. God, she was so beautiful. Wide eyes. Mahogany skin. And full lips. She had her whole life ahead of her still. But she allowed him to ruin it. And I couldn't save her. My chest tightens as I think about her. "I'm sorry I couldn't save you, Mom. But I promise I will save her."

ZARA

I hate attending these parties with Tristan. It's a bunch of people wearing expensive clothing and standing around discussing politics. But the Mayor's Ball is important to him. He's lining up all his allies before he announces his bid for the governor's seat. My arm is looped through his. I'm wearing a gold cocktail dress that I designed myself. My makeup is flawless, and I've been wearing a smile all night. Pretending to be happy. "Zara, it's so good to see you again."

The current governor kisses my hand. "Tristan, she gets more beautiful every time I see her."

"Thank you."

He releases my hand and places his eyes on Tristan. "Still trying to convince me to give you my support, huh?"

"I think it would be in your best interest to support me. And the state of Georgia's."

"That's where you're wrong. Word on the street is that if you get elected, you plan to undo everything I worked hard for. You want to reduce the budget by cutting jobs?"

"They're jobs that aren't needed."

"Every job is needed."

"Really? Office Ambassador?"

He shrugs. "She runs the office for me."

"She's your sister. She makes over a hundred grand, as a secretary. Governor, you're creating unnecessary positions for your friends and family and paying them six figures or more. I think it's time we eliminate those positions and give that money back to the state of Georgia."

And that's my queue. "Excuse me, gentlemen. I need to use the ladies' room."

Tristan kisses my cheek before I leave him to talk politics. I use the restroom, then head to the bar and request a glass of red wine. The bartender slides the glass toward me. I thank him before I turn around to find Tristan. He's still talking to the governor, but someone else has joined them. I take a sip as I watch the tall blonde bat her eyes and place her hand on Tristan's shoulder as she laughs. I sip some more as I watch his eyes drag down to the tits that spill out of her too small dress. They're flirting with each other. A normal wife would be upset. A normal wife would march over there, drag the hussy by her hair, and show her what happens when you flirt with someone else's husband. But I'm not a normal wife. And what Tristan and I have isn't a normal marriage. So, I watch from afar without feeling an ounce of jealousy.

Tristan closes my door and drunkenly rounds the hood of the car. The smell of liquor fills the inside as soon as he slides in. He and the Governor must have put their differences aside because they were drinking together and acting like best friends by the end of the night. He slams his door shut. "Governor Dillan is an asshole."

"I thought you two settled your differences."

"Well, you thought wrong."

He starts the car, and I watch the other couples stagger from the building. "You know, you could have had my back in there."

"Had your back how? I did what you told me to do. Look pretty and be quiet. Remember?"

The wine helps me find my voice. The voice I buried deep when Tristan started abusing me. "What did you say?"

"Nothing. I just meant that I didn't think you wanted me interfering in your work conversations."

He leans back in his seat. "That's right. But I didn't want you over at the bar flirting with the bartender either."

I have no idea what he's talking about. I said about three words to the bartender the entire time I sat there. "I wasn't flirting with the bartender, Tristan."

"You think I don't know what the fuck you were doing? I saw you smiling at him."

"If anybody was flirting, it was you. You were the one with the blonde hanging all over you."

He looks at me like he can't believe I said it. Like how dare I talk back to him. He chose the wrong night to pick a fight with me. I'm tired. My feet hurt from these stupid, too-small heels he bought for me, and the wine is still fueling through my system. "I think you forgot who the fuck you're talking to."

I know exactly who the fuck I'm talking to. And I don't care.

He must have heard my thoughts because he slaps me so hard my head turns. I grab my face, massaging out some of the sting. "Get out."

"What?"

"You heard me. Get the fuck out. You can find your own ride home since you know so much."

"But Tristan, it's late."

"Either you get out willingly, or I drag you out myself."

I shake my head. "Fine."

I open the door and step outside of the car. It's just my luck the rain starts as soon as my feet hit the pavement. Once I close the door, Tristan speeds off. I watch the car turn the corner through tears. That fucking bastard. It's dark. It's late. And it's raining. I place my clutch on top of my head, checking my surroundings, seeking cover from the rain. I jog carefully to the bus stop on the corner. I pull my phone out of my clutch and notice I have one new message. From Tyson, asking if I'm okay. The answer enters my mind almost instantly. Should I ask him to pick me up? I shake my head. No. I can't involve him in my personal life. But he said to come to him if I ever need anything. Judging by the men who walk by and watch me suspiciously, I need safety right now. I didn't bring any money with me or my bank card because my clutch was barely big enough to hold my phone. And since I was with Tristan, I didn't think I needed it. Tears spill as I realize I don't have any other choice. My fingers move rapidly as I type out the message.

Me: I'm not okay. I'm stranded.

The phone rings before I can put it back in my purse. "Hi."

"Where are you?"

"I'm at the corner of the Renaissance Building. I'm at the bus stop."

"I'll be right there."

I expected him to ask questions, but he didn't. I place my phone back inside my clutch and wait patiently. Ten minutes later, a man walks by and stops when he sees me at the bus stop. He's tall in stature and heavy-set. He's wearing a fatigue jacket and carrying a duffel bag. "Need any company?"

"No. I'm okay, thank you."

He looks me up and down like a piece of candy. "What's a pretty girl like you doing out here all alone?"

"I'm waiting for my husband. He went to get the car around the corner. He'll be here any minute now."

He looks around, then steps closer. "Give me your purse."

"I don't have any money."

He removes a blade from his pocket. "Hand it over, lady."

TYSON

I find Zara just in time. It's raining hard, but not so hard that I can't see a man standing too close to her. I'm out of the car before it's barely in Park. I yank him away with force. He tries to stab me with a knife, but I block it and grab his arm, twisting it behind him. He's bigger than me, but I'm stronger. I'm able to slam him down on the ground, and the knife falls from his grip. I pin him down. "Get in the car," I yell to Zara over the rain.

I watch her sprint past me, and once I hear the car door slam, I grab the knife beside me and place it against his throat. "You get off by hurting women?"

His eyes grow wide with fear. "Please, I wasn't going to hurt her. I only wanted to scare her for her purse."

"Oh, so you like to hurt and steal from women."

"No. I swear. Please don't kill me."

I want to slice his throat. I want him to bleed out on the sidewalk for even *thinking* about hurting her. But I don't kill him. I take the knife and cut just enough to produce blood. The rain is pounding so hard, it washes the blood away in seconds. "If you *ever* think about hurting a woman again, I will find you and finish the job, do you understand?"

He nods frantically. I rise to my feet, knife still in hand, and jerk my head to the side. "Get the fuck out of here."

He scrambles to his feet and runs off. I toss the knife and quickly walk to my car. I slide inside, not caring that I'm soaking my leather seats. My only concern is Zara. "Are you okay?"

She nods. She's drenched, and her hands are trembling. I turn the heat up and reach for a blanket in the back seat. "I knew you might need this."

She smiles as she takes it from me and wraps it around herself. "What were you doing out here alone this late?" My tone is sharp. I don't mean to sound angry, but she should know better. Atlanta is a beautiful city. But it has its fair share of criminals roaming the streets at night. She could have gotten hurt, or worse, she could have gotten herself killed. The car is quiet as I wait for her to answer me. "Zara…"

She turns around to face me. Her eyes are red and swollen. "Tristan. He left me here."

That's it. This is the last straw. There's no way I'm going to let this slide. Tristan considers me a friend, and no real friend would allow him to do something so stupid and get away with it. "Tell me what happened."

"We attended the Mayor's Ball tonight. We were about to go home when he got upset with me and kicked me out of the car."

"What could possibly upset him so much that he would kick you out of the car, especially this late at night?"

She shakes her head. "He thought I was flirting with the bartender."

I take a deep breath and grip the steering wheel. "Zara, you do know that isn't normal, right? He's your husband. He should be protecting you, not putting you in harm's way."

I had to ask. Sometimes women who are victims make excuses. They think it's their fault that they're being mistreated. I need to know where her head is at before I decide how I'm going to handle this. She nods. "Of course, I know that."

I put the car in drive. "Good. Because I'm not going to let him get away with this."

I see the panic in her face before I pull onto the street. "Tyson, no, you can't."

"Why not? He left you out on the fucking street like some animal."

"You don't understand."

"What is there to understand other than the fact you could have gotten hurt?"

She grows quiet before she replies. "Tyson, I don't expect you to get it. But I need to deal with this in my own way."

"Your own way. Will this be before or after you end up in the hospital? Or maybe dead in the ground. I know how this stuff works."

She turns her head and looks out her window as I drive. Maybe I shouldn't have said it. Maybe I came on too strong. It's her life, and I have no right trying to tell her what to do. She speaks softly. "Just, please don't get involved. It'll make things worse. And…" She turns back around to face me. "He'll make me quit. I don't want to stop working for you. I have a plan. Just trust me and let me handle this."

I park around the corner to avoid Tristan seeing Zara get out of my car. I hate this. All of it. We argued back and forth for ten minutes before I agreed not to pull into her driveway. But I made it clear that I would wait until I knew she was inside. She removes the blanket and places it on the back seat. "Thank you."

I don't want her to leave. Her makeup is smudged, her hair is wet and unruly, but she's so beautiful. Her wet dress clings to her, and her nipples hardened once she removed the blanket. She looks like a work of art. How could Tristan ever mistreat her? "I don't like this, Zara."

"I'll be fine."

"Let me take you to a hotel tonight where you'll be safe. Let him cool off before you go back in there."

She shakes her head. "Thanks for offering, but I'll be okay."

I take a deep breath. "Will you text me as soon as you get inside? Then again to let me know you're safe?"

She doesn't answer me. Instead, she watches me curiously.

She places her palm on the side of my cheek and smiles. "You're a good man, Tyson."

I place my hand around hers, and my pulse quickens at the warmth of her skin. What comes next is unexpected. I pull her to me and place my lips on hers. I didn't think before I did it. I just reacted the way my body commanded me to. Her lips open slightly, allowing me to explore further with my tongue. Her lips are soft, and I start to wonder how the rest of her body feels. But I don't get the chance to find out. She pulls her lips from mine and watches me with sad eyes. "Why do you care about what happens to me?"

I take her hand in mine. "I don't need a reason. I just do."

I didn't get to sleep until the wee hours of the morning. Once Zara texted me that she was safe, I took a ride to clear my thoughts. I said I would remain professional, but I crossed the line anyway. Now I'm hoping I didn't drive her away. She begged me not to mention to Tristan that I gave her a ride home. I reluctantly agreed and now, I feel like I'm adding to the problem by condoning his behavior. I walk into the kitchen as Charlie adds sliced mango to her smoothie. "Late night?"

I take a seat at the table and reach for my mail. "Yeah."

She pours in a little bit of pineapple juice. "Where did you run off to so late?"

"I needed to put out a few fires. I took a drive after that to clear my mind."

I feel horrible lying to her. I feel even worse that she has no idea I kissed another woman last night. I promised her a night of passionate sex. She wore something sexy to bed for me. But just as I got out of the shower, my phone buzzed with an incoming text from Zara. I had to rush off, leaving Charlie horny and frustrated. This isn't like us. I might not be in love with her, but sex has never been an issue for us. We had great sex. Lot's of it. But lately, I don't desire her. "I'm leaving for New York."

"Booked another client?"

"Yup. That up and coming actress Tina Lily hired me to do her makeup for The Today Show. She has an interview and wants to look her best."

"That's good news."

"I know. I'm hoping she recommends me to more of her celebrity friends."

"I'm sure she will."

I stand and grab my coffee. Eager to go upstairs and get ready for work. "Oh, I finished the list. We'll need invitations for four hundred seventy people."

I nod. "Okay. I'll look at it later."

CHAPTER 8

ZARA

I'm nervous about seeing Tyson today. I thought about him all night. The way his lips tasted against mine. The way he watched me like he wanted to strip me bare. Tristan was out cold on the couch when I got in. I crept upstairs, took a nice hot shower, and touched myself as I thought about Tyson. He saved me from being attacked last night. He was my hero, and it turned me on something fierce. I imagined his hands roaming my body as I made myself come twice. I shake my head as I fill the water pitcher with ice. What the hell am I doing? He's about to be married. I can't have him. Or can I? If he didn't want me, why would he kiss me? Why would he worry about me? "You're overthinking it."

I spin around and come face to face with him. "What do you mean?"

He takes a step forward and speaks in a low voice. "You're wondering if I regret kissing you last night."

I nod. "Yeah, I am."

We're quiet as a few people pass us and pile into the conference room. When the coast is clear, he leans in and speaks into my ear. "The answer is no."

He walks away, and I fill the pitcher with water. I leave the kitchen and carry it to the conference room where our morning meeting is about to start. I place the water in the center of the table and take a seat to the far right. The room grows quiet as Tyson walks in. How is it possible for him to look so damn sexy this early? He's not wearing a tie today. Just a blue and black shirt, with the top button opened. I get a whiff of his cologne as he walks by. "Don't even think about it," Pam whispers to me. "We've all tried, but he's not interested in the help."

He takes his seat. "Pam, is there something you need to say to the group?"

His eyes dart between the two of us. "No. I was just asking Zara how she's doing so far."

His jawline tightens. "Let's focus, please."

The meeting adjourns, and I can't help but think about Pam's words. She's right. I'm the help. What could Tyson possibly see in me? He's rich. Filthy rich. He has a successful career and can have any woman he wants. Which explains why he's engaged to a woman as beautiful as Charlie. He has it all. I head straight to my office and notice I have a notification on my phone. It's a text message.

Tristan: I'm sorry about last night.

"Message from Tristan?"

I jump at the sound of Tyson's voice. "Yeah. How'd you know?"

He nods toward the phone I'm holding. "Whatever message you were reading, you didn't look happy."

I place the phone down on my desk as he walks inside. "We should talk."

He walks over to my window and shoves his hands in his pockets. He speaks with his back turned to me. "Did Pam say something to upset you in the meeting?"

66

I fold my arms. "Why do you ask?"

He chuckles. "Because you looked upset."

"She said they've all made advances at you, but you weren't interested in the help."

He turns around and smirks. "First, I don't consider any of my employees as *the help*. Second, I just wasn't interested in any of them, especially Pam." He takes two long strides toward me. "I've never cheated on Charlie." He searches my eyes. "Until last night."

"Why? Why now?"

"I'm drawn to you. I can't stop thinking about you, worrying about you. No matter how much I try to stop it."

"Tyson, you don't even know me."

"Which is why none of this makes any fucking sense."

He looks frustrated with himself. Angry even. "Since we're being honest, I didn't regret kissing you either. Tyson, the way you protected me last night made me feel safe. And that's something I haven't felt in a long time." He watches me as I continue. "But it doesn't change the fact that I'm married. And although I have plans to change that as soon as I can, it won't change the fact that you're about to marry Charlie."

His head drops as I say her name. "You're right. And you deserve better. Better than Tristan. And better than what I did last night."

"What do you mean?"

"I mean you were vulnerable. Scared. Kissing you should have been the last thing on my mind. Except it wasn't. And for that, I'm sorry."

"Don't apologize. I kissed you back, remember."

He chuckles. "How could I forget? I know I barely know you, Zara. But I see the side of you that you try to hide. I know there's more to you than what Tristan gives you credit for. My gut is telling me to keep you close, and my gut is never wrong.

I've relied on it throughout my career. It's how I got to where I am."

I blush. "Thank you. That's very sweet of you."

"I'm only speaking the truth."

The air shifts between us. Causing a magnetic pull that neither of us acts on. His feet stay planted in place, and I stay seated at my desk. I want to reach out to him. I want to sink into his embrace. I want him to hold me tight while he whispers the things he just said to me again and again. But I can't. We've both just acknowledged that the kiss we shared was wrong. I need to forget it ever happened and move on. He breaks the silence. "Can you promise me that if you ever feel like your life is in danger, you'll call me? I promise I'll take you straight to safety and it'll remain confidential."

I don't get a chance to answer him because his cell phone rings. He looks at the caller and then up at me. His eyes narrow as he answers the phone. "Tristan, to what do I owe the pleasure?"

My heart beats fast when I hear his name. My palm grows sweaty at the thought of him calling Tyson. Did he somehow find out that Tyson brought me home last night? "Sure, I'll see you then."

He ends the call and shoves the phone back into his pocket. "What did he want?"

"He wants to meet up for drinks later."

"Are you going?"

"Yeah. I'm going."

"Are you sure it's a good idea?"

"Yeah, I won't mention anything about us. Do you trust me?"

I hardly know him, but so far, he's proved that he's honest and that he cares. I nod. "Yes. I trust you."

TYSON

I watch Tristan's eyes follow the redhead. He's stared at every ass that's walked past us. He's pathetic. He has a beautiful wife at home, yet it isn't enough for him. I could tell Zara was uneasy about me meeting Tristan for drinks, but what was I supposed to do, say no? It would look suspicious. And since she's sworn me to secrecy, I must play the part until I know for sure she's out of Tristan's grip. One false move right now, and he'll forbid her to work for me or even talk to me. And that wouldn't be good for either of us. "Are you sure you want to get married, man? I mean, look at what you'll be giving up committing to one woman."

I shrug as I drink my beer. "I've had my share of women, Tristan. It gets old after a while."

He takes a bite of a French fry. "Yeah, but wives get old too."

I turn to face him. "Is Zara getting old to you?"

I'm taking a risk here by asking about her. But he's the one who brought up the topic of women, so I might as well get as much information as I can. "I guess you could say that. We were young when we got married."

"Do you love her?"

"Yeah. I love her. But…"

"But what?"

He picks his beer up and takes a swig. "It's complicated, Tyson. And she works for you now, so the topic of our marriage is off limits."

I raise my hands in surrender. "Hey, man, you're the one bringing up marriage and women. Not me."

He laughs out loud. "Fair point. Anyway, I'm glad you're back. I could use a friend right now."

A friend? I'm not his friend. And I want to tell him this. But I won't break Zara's trust. I won't make things worse for her.

Men like Tristan need to be taught a lesson, and as soon as I'm able, I'll make sure that he learns his.

It's late when I get in, and Charlie's up, reading a wedding magazine. I was supposed to come home early and go over the guest list she prepared, but I didn't. I can tell she's not happy about it, but I'm not in the mood to argue with her. She looks at the clock. "You were supposed to be here hours ago."

"I'm sorry. I lost track of time."

"Tyson, is there something you want to talk about? You don't seem like yourself lately."

This is my chance. This is my chance to tell her the truth. But it's late. And I'm mentally exhausted. "Just stress from work, that's all."

"When is the fashion show?"

"It's next week."

"Good. I'll be glad when it's over so we can finally focus on our wedding."

I ignore her statement and remove my clothes. "I'm going to take a shower."

I enter the bathroom and turn the shower on. I step inside and allow the water to stream down my face and relax my anxiety. Images of Zara in that emerald dress flash into my mind. Those hips. That high split that showed her thigh. My dick hardens, and I massage it slowly. I think about the kiss we shared and how soft her lips are. Fantasies creep into my mind as I stroke myself. I think about my lips between her thighs. Her moans filling my ears. I'm stroking faster now as I think about how good it would feel to be buried inside her. I'm close. So fucking close to coming all over the shower wall. My head drops back with pleasure as I think about her screaming my name. I'm so hard right now it hurts. I grit my teeth as I'm about to come. I stroke myself faster. As soon as I'm about to release, the shower door swings open. "Tyson!"

"What the fuck, Charlie?"

"Are you seriously jerking off in the shower?"

I turn off the water, grab a towel, and wrap it around myself. "Can I have some fucking privacy?"

"I was about to join you. I was going to give you a blowjob in the shower, but I guess you've already pleased yourself."

It takes me a second to realize she's completely naked. Shit! I've screwed up big time. She grabs her bathrobe, slides it on, and crosses her arms. "I'll sleep in the guest room tonight."

The next day is awkward between me and Charlie. We had a prior engagement that I couldn't cancel, even though I wanted to. "You're all set. Prenups are never easy, but I'm glad you two could figure it out."

"I'll be well taken care of during the marriage anyway, so I didn't mind signing it," Charlie replies.

I nod and stand. "Thank you, Justin."

Justin is my lawyer. But he's also a friend. I don't make any business decisions without running them past him first. He shakes me and Charlie's hand, and we exit his office. Charlie's been quiet all day, and I can't say that I blame her. She's been throwing herself at me for days, and I've been finding every excuse not to sleep with her. I can only imagine how it made her feel when she caught me jerking off like a teenaged boy. "You okay?" I ask as I start the car.

"I don't know, Tyson. My fiancé would rather jerk off than have sex with me. So, you tell me, should I be okay?"

Yup, she's pissed.

"I'm sorry. It just happened. I was cleaning it, and it got hard. I didn't want to bother you because it was late."

"It gets hard in the shower, but not when I wrap my lips around it. Something is seriously wrong with that picture."

I decide I won't win this argument, so I let it go. "I'm sorry."

She ignores me. She turns the music up and doesn't say a word for the remainder of the drive. When we arrive home, she stomps upstairs, and I head to the kitchen to pour myself a drink. It isn't fair how I'm treating Charlie. She deserves the truth. I do care about her feelings and don't want to hurt her. This has gone far enough. And I must end it. But it'll have to wait. If I end things now, she'll make a scene and it'll be a distraction. A distraction I don't need before the fashion show. So, I make the decision to tell her afterwards. Once the show is over, I'll tell her what we both know to be true. That we shouldn't be getting married.

I've worked side by side with Zara for the past week and it's been great. Her ideas are refreshing. Her energy is contagious. It's been just me and her in my office for hours every day. I've brushed my hand against hers. I've sat closely to her. But I managed to stay professional. "Well, it's getting late. I better get home."

"Thanks for your help, Zara. I think we have everything we need."

"I think we pulled it together nicely."

"Thanks to you."

"I can't take the credit. Everything was mostly in place before you hired me."

"Yeah, but it wasn't as efficient. You stepped in and made a huge difference. Thank you."

She stands and smiles. "Thanks for taking a chance on me. This past week really showed me that I belong in fashion."

"I knew it from your first day. Come on, I'll walk you out."

I follow her to the door, and she spins around when we reach it. "Thank you for, um...also keeping it professional. You said you wouldn't mix business with pleasure, and you didn't. Thank you for keeping your word."

I swallow hard. "It hasn't been easy."

She blinks a few times. "It hasn't?"

"No. As a matter of fact, it's killing me not to kiss you right now."

A tiny gasp escapes her mouth. I can't tell if she's shocked or horrified. I place both hands at the side of her. Caging her in. "I need to kiss you, Zara."

She nods. "Okay."

She wraps her arms around my neck as my lips claim hers. I tried. I really tried to do the right thing. When she walked away, I tried my best not to stare. Every time she got close, I forced myself not to look down at her breasts. And when she threw her head back with laughter, I swore I wouldn't focus on those lips I once tasted. But with all the self-restraint I practiced this week, it didn't help. I still wanted her. I needed to taste her lips on mine once again. I turn her around and unzip the back of her dress. I place small kisses on her upper back. The dress falls to the floor, and she's left wearing blue lace panties and no bra. My hand moves to the front of her. "Do you want me to stop?" I ask as I place my hand on her center.

"No."

I slip my hand inside her panties, where I find her wet and steamy. My dick is instantly hard. I slide her panties down, and she places her hands firmly against the door. She steps out of them and kicks them to the side. I take a step back. I shed my shirt and pants quickly before I bring myself close behind her. "Last chance, Zara."

She spins around in my arms. "You're ruining the mood."

I smirk right before I lift her up. I hold her in place as I slide inside her. She grips me tighter as I move in and out. I hold her with ease, and my stamina never wavers as my strokes go deeper and deeper. Her moans echo in my office, and as much as I try to hold back. I can't. I moan with her. I tell her how good she feels. How I've been fantasizing about her since the moment I laid eyes on her. When I tell her how hard she's made me, she digs her nails firmly into my back and releases around me. Three more strokes, and I cry out with pleasure as I come. I stay still for a moment before I slide out and gently lower her to her feet. I search her eyes for any hint that she regrets what we just did. For any sign that this was a mistake. But I don't see any. She smiles. "Tyson, that was…"

"I know. It was the same for me."

I bend down to gather her clothing. "You can use my bathroom to clean yourself."

She nods but doesn't move. Her expression changes, and that look I was searching for is there now. The look of regret. "What's wrong?"

"What we just did, it wasn't right."

Her words hit me like a ton of bricks. The last thing I want is for her to regret what we've just done. "It didn't feel that way to me."

"But what happens now? What about Tristan? What about Charlie?"

She's panicking, so I try my best to calm her. I lean in and kiss her softly on the lips. "Nothing will change between us, and if Tristan is a problem for you, I can get you away from him."

She's quiet for a moment before she asks her next question. "And what about Charlie?"

I take a deep breath. "Things aren't what they seem, Zara."

CHAPTER 9

ZARA

It's the big night. The night of the fashion show, and I'm so nervous. I run from room to room, checking on every detail. I need to make sure the models are ready. That the DJ has the correct music selection for each showcase. And most importantly, I need to make sure that there are zero mistakes. Tonight must be perfect. Tristan was supposed to join me, but luckily, he got called away for an important work function, so I came alone. I'm glad though. I don't need him spewing his negativity tonight and breathing down my neck when I'm already a nervous wreck. I'm fixing the tie on one of the models when I see *him*. He stands tall with confidence as he surveys the area. He's wearing a black suit, a gold shirt, and a gold and black tie. His eyes meet mine, and he smiles at me from across the room. I take one last look at the model before I walk toward him. "Hey."

"Hey, everything looks good."

"Yup, everything is in order and ready to go."

"You look beautiful tonight."

"Thank you. And you look handsome."

He looks behind me. "No Tristan?"

I shake my head. "No. He got called away for work. He's not into this kind of stuff anyway."

He nods, then takes a step closer. "Can I see you after the show?"

"I'm not sure if that's a good idea."

"It's a great idea."

"Tyson, I…"

I'm interrupted when Charlie walks in. "There you are," she says as she takes her rightful place next to him. "I've been looking all over for you."

He swings his gaze to her. "I needed to come backstage and check on a few things."

Her eyes land on me, and she looks me up and down. "I'm sure Zara can take care of things back here. I mean, isn't that why you hired her?"

He narrows his eyes and clenches his jaw tightly. "This is my brand, Charlie. She shouldn't have to do this alone."

The show was a success. Every model graciously walked the runway, showcasing Tyson's suits. The crowd loved them, and by the end of the night, he agreed to five meetings to discuss purchasing orders. I sit down on the couch, kick my shoes off, and rub my feet as the last model exits the dressing room. I close my eyes and smile. My first major fashion show, and I delivered. Clapping noises interrupt me. My eyes pop open and land on Tyson. "You did amazing work, Zara. You exceeded my expectations."

I drop my foot to the ground. "Thank you."

"You were right about the colored suits. It left them wanting more by debuting only a few. I had two companies approach me about carrying my brand in their fall lineup."

"Tyson, that's good news."

"Yeah, it is. Do you need a ride home?"

I shake my head. "No. I'm supposed to call Tristan when I'm ready. He's picking me up."

Displeasure crosses his face. "Hmm."

"Where's Charlie?"

"My driver took her home. I told her I needed to finish up here."

"Well, I've taken care of everything already."

"I know. I needed to see you."

"Tyson..."

He interrupts me when he drops to his knees in front of me. "I thought about you all night." He pushes me down on my back and slides the bottom of my black silk dress up and around my waist. He slightly separates my thighs. "I couldn't get you out of my mind." In one swift pull, he rips my black thong and kisses my folds softly. "Couldn't get *this* out of my mind."

I look down at him with lust-filled eyes. "We shouldn't be doing this." My voice is shaky when I say it. Lacking the confidence needed to sound believable.

He chuckles. "Zara, *this* is exactly what we should be doing."

I grab the edge of the couch as his tongue teases me. "Tyson..."

"Relax. Let me please you right now."

I spread my legs wider, allowing him full access to my most intimate part. I wriggle beneath him as he licks me. "Oh god..."

He licks faster. Sucks harder. Pleasing all my sensitive spots. I try hard to hold on. I try my best to savor this moment. It feels too good to end so quickly. "Tyson, I'm close."

I see bright lights behind my closed eyelids. My body buckles, and my thighs clench around his ears as I come. I whimper as he pulls his mouth away. He stands to his feet. "Take your dress off."

The dress I made is light. Simple. And can easily be removed.

As he undresses himself, I slide the spaghetti straps off my shoulders and slide it above my head. I'm completely naked as I lie before him. His eyes rake my body before his lips attack mine. Our tongues tangle as his hands softly caress my loose curls. He pulls his lips away. "Tell me you want me, Zara."

I nod. "Yes. Yes, I want you."

He's inside me as soon as the words leave my mouth. Filling me quickly. My hands roam his washboard chest and strong back as he strokes me deep. He alternates between kissing me on the neck and kissing me on the lips. He claims my body as if it belongs to him. "Fuck, you feel good."

My mouth opens to say the same. To tell him how good he feels. But the words don't come out. A moan escapes in place of them. My thighs open wider as I wrap my legs around him. My eyes meet his, and I'm done for. His strokes speed up as he watches me intensely. Heat pools in my belly, and I speak for the first time since he's been inside me. "Right there. Don't stop."

He smirks as he keeps the momentum going. His eyes bore into mine. "That's right. Let go, baby."

I grip his forearm tightly as I release. Crying out and not caring if someone hears. "Shit, Zara..."

I feel him spill inside me before his body locks in place. He relaxes and gently moves a piece of hair out of my face before he kisses me. When he pulls his lips from mine, he continues to stare at me. "I'll never regret touching you."

I wrap my arms around his neck. "Neither will I."

Tyson gave us all a bonus for our hard work on the fashion show. He also gave us the day off on Monday, so we have a three-day weekend. He said he wants us to rest before returning to work. That might be the case for his other employees, but not for me. I get no rest in this house. I got up early this morning to clean and cook breakfast before Tristan woke up. He was in a horrible mood last night when he picked me up. He was pissed that he had to leave his event to bring me home. He said that this arrangement isn't working for him anymore and he thinks it's best if I quit. I said nothing. I stared out my window with teary eyes. I was angry. I'm working hard to prove myself, and I dare him try to snatch away all my hard work. By the end of the night, he changed his mind again and said I could keep the job. He enters the kitchen just as I finish making his plate. "You're up early."

I plaster on a smile. "Yeah. Wanted to make your favorite this morning. To thank you for picking me up last night."

He takes a seat at the table. "It's nice to feel appreciated."

He takes a bite of his eggs Benedict as I place a glass of cranberry juice beside him. "I saw you got your first paycheck."

"Yes, I did."

"It's not as much as I thought it would be. I thought the purpose of you working was to pull your weight around here."

It's not as much as he thought it would be because I arranged for *some* of my money to be deposited into the account we share. I secretly opened a separate checking account, and the rest of my money is deposited into that one. I also had my bonus check deposited there. "My next one should be more. I started in the middle of the pay week."

He takes a sip of his juice. "It's warm."

I grab the glass and put a few more ice cubes in it before placing it back beside him. "We've been invited to Tyson's for dinner tonight."

"Okay."

"And wear something nice."

"Got it."

He rises from his chair, leaving his half-eaten dish behind. "I'll see you later."

∾

I didn't put too much effort into my outfit for tonight, but Tristan won't know the difference. He never does—he just talks a good game. I honestly wasn't in the mood to put something super nice together. My mind is occupied with thoughts of Tyson. Why didn't he tell me he invited us over for dinner? I still throb from the feel of him. I can still smell him. Images of him tasting me make me wet. My phone buzzes with an incoming message.

Tyson: You didn't text me back last night.

I couldn't text him back. Tristan was on me like a drill sergeant and would have noticed that I was texting him.

Me: I'm sorry. But I'm okay. Why didn't you tell me about the dinner tonight?

Tyson: I thought Tristan told you.

Me: No. He didn't. But don't you think it's a bit much?

Tyson: No.

Me: It's going to be awkward. Tristan will know something is up.

Tyson: No, he won't. I need to talk to you, Zara. Things aren't what you think they are.

Me: I can't do this, Tyson. You're engaged, and my situation is complicated.

Tyson: Just let me explain before you decide.

Me: There's nothing to explain. I have a plan and can't afford the distraction right now. We need to be professional from now on. Please understand.

I turn my phone off and place it in my purse before I give him the chance to respond. What was he thinking, inviting us over? I pull the white silk blouse from the hanger and smile. This blouse was a gift from Tristan. I've never worn it before, and holding it now reminds me of the good times. The times when he showed me that he loved me. Times where he brought home flowers for no reason and kissed me tenderly every night before bed. My smile quickly disappears as the memories take a turn for the worse. I think about the name calling. The physical abuse and the control he has over me. My eyes swell with tears. Maybe I should have done what my parents wanted me to do, then I wouldn't be in this position. Did my stubbornness push me into the arms of an abuser? Maybe there's still time. Maybe I don't have to save enough money before I can leave. I grab my phone and pull the contact up for my parents. My finger pauses over the number as I take a deep breath, deciding if I should call. I push the *Call* button. My father answers.

"Zara?"

"Hi, Daddy."

"I'm surprised to hear from you."

I ignore his comment. "How's Mom?"

"She's doing well. She's out in the garden right now."

There's a moment of silence before he speaks. "You must want something, so spit it out."

"I was wondering if I could borrow some money. I just got an amazing job, but it'll take me a while to save. I promise I'll pay you back."

"Let me get this straight. I offer you the keys to the kingdom so you can have a better life. You turn me down to chase after some clothing dream, and now you call me asking for money?"

"No, I'm asking for a loan. You can even add interest."

"What about your husband?"

"He doesn't know about this."

"I see. I've never met the man since we didn't get a wedding invite."

"You know why I didn't invite you."

"Yet you invited your Aunt Maggie. Jesus, you barely knew her, and she's your great aunt, at that."

"I called to ask you for a loan. Why are we discussing my wedding?"

"Because I thought you had good enough sense to marry

someone who could provide. Seems I've failed you as a parent once again."

"Please, Dad, this is important. Can I borrow the money?"

"No."

"What?"

"I said no. This is the life you chose. The life you wanted. You had your chance to have a better one, but you threw that chance away. So, figure it out on your own."

"But Dad..."

"My answer is no. And Zara?"

"Yes."

"You shouldn't keep secrets from your husband. I thought we raised you better than that."

The line disconnects, and I plop down on the bed, feeling defeated. Why did I bother calling? I knew I would be on my own the minute I was kicked out of the house. I have no one but myself. I need to do whatever is necessary to get out of this marriage. A tear slides down my cheek as the front door slams. "Zara!" Tristan yells

I wipe away my tears. "I'm upstairs."

He walks into the room. "You're not dressed yet."

"Sorry, I was looking for something to wear. Give me an hour, okay, honey?"

Tyson's home is stunning. The foyer boasts a double staircase, a crystal chandelier, and shiny hardwood floors. My hand is intertwined with Tristan's as we enter. "Tyson sure is living well," he whispers in my ear.

Tyson walks down the stairs, and I almost faint. I've seen him in suits. Shirts and ties. But I've never seen him look like this. He's wearing a pair of dark denim jeans and a white polo shirt. He looks relaxed. Comfortable. And good enough to eat. "Zara. Tristan. I'm glad you guys could make it."

He and Tristan do their manly handshake. "Tyson, this place is huge. I had no idea you were living *this* good."

Tyson chuckles. "Thanks, man."

"You have a lovely home," I add.

Charlie rounds the corner. "Thank you. I picked this place out myself."

Envy rushes through me as she rests her hand on Tyson's shoulder. "This place is state of the art. A pool, sauna, tennis court, IMAX theatre—"

Tristan interrupts her. "Wait a minute, you have an IMAX theatre? I *have* to see it."

Charlie smiles. "Come on, I'll show you. Zara, can I steal your husband for a second?"

Her choice of words is fitting. I nod. "Sure."

Once they disappear around the corner, Tyson grabs my elbow gently. "We need to talk."

CHAPTER 10

TYSON

Charlie has become increasingly irritating, and I honestly don't know how much more I can take. I was supposed to break things off with her right after the fashion show, but she found out one of her former clients died, and I didn't want to add to her grief. When my eyes landed on Zara from the stair-well, I wanted to snatch her hand out of Tristan's and make her mine. The white blouse she's wearing fits snuggly. The denim jeans hug her hips and thighs. Her hair is simple. Swooped in a ponytail. But she looks beautiful. I need to explain my situation to her. I need to let her know that she isn't the reason I'm ending my engagement to Charlie. She needs to know why I'm so fiercely protective of her. "You want to talk now?"

"Yes, it can't wait."

She snatches her arm away, "Tyson, this wasn't a good idea. Why did you have us come here tonight knowing what happened between us?"

"Charlie is leaving for New York in the morning for a job.

This dinner was already planned. I thought Tristan told you about it."

She shakes her head. "No, he didn't."

"Zara, I told him about it the other night."

She looks surprised. "Oh."

"I need to tell you—"

She interrupts me. "Tyson, we can't be together."

"Why not?"

"I'm married."

"Unhappily and planning to leave. Next reason."

"You're engaged."

"That's actually what I want to talk to you about—"

Charlie's laugh interrupts me, and I take a step back from Zara. "You two are still standing here?"

"Yeah, we were just discussing work."

"Well, let's not discuss work tonight. Let's eat."

She leads everyone into the dining room, and we take our seats. My mouth waters at the spread of food on the table. Stuffed flounder, shrimp scampi, lobster tails, jasmine rice, potatoes, and veggies. All cooked by me. "This smell's so good," Zara compliments.

"Tyson does most of the cooking. He prepared my favorites tonight."

"That's one thing Zar can do. She knows how to make a hell of a meal," Tristan states as he places a scoop of potatoes on his plate.

There's a hell of a lot more Zara can do besides cook. But Tristan can't see it because he's too busy putting her down to make himself look good.

"How long have you two been married?" Charlie asks.

"Two years," Zara answers.

"Wow, I can't wait until I walk down that aisle and marry Tyson. He's the love of my life."

Zara glances at me, and I think I'm going to vomit. Love of

her life? Charlie knows we're far from soul mates. Zara narrows her eyes. "When is the big day, Charlie?"

"We haven't set a date yet. Tyson's been so busy with the fashion show. But now that it's over, we can start wedding planning."

Sadness flashes in Zara's eyes. "I'm sure you're both eager to get started."

This is ridiculous. I can't let Charlie sit here and pretend we're the perfect couple who's hopelessly in love. I change the subject. "Tristan, are you nervous about announcing your candidacy for governor?"

"Nope. I'm the best man for the job, so I know I'll have the people's vote."

"What's your political agenda?"

"Gentlemen, please. Zara and I aren't interested in hearing about politics, right, Zara?"

Zara's eyes widen with fear. Charlie doesn't know that her answer could cause Tristan to hurt her. I jump in quickly before she has a chance to reply. "You're right, Charlie. No politics, and no work. Let's toast to a night of drinks, laughter, and fun."

We've been at the table laughing for hours. The ladies drank wine while Tristan and I drank beers. Tristan and I laughed about our college days, and for a moment, I got a glimpse of the man I used to know. I tried my hardest to keep my eyes off Zara. It's refreshing to see her drinking and laughing, having a good time. When Tristan starts to talk about all the women we slept with in college, I stop him. "Okay. I think it's time to call it a night."

He laughs. "What's the matter, Tyson? Are you ashamed of being a man whore?"

"We were young. And that was a long time ago."

Tristan laughs. "Yeah, but they were the good ole days." He stands to his feet. "This was fun. We should do it again."

"Definitely. We'll be like family soon anyway," Charlie adds.

I stand as well. "I'll walk you guys out."

We reach the front door, and Zara spins around. "Thank you, guys, for having us over."

I nod, disappointed that I didn't get to tell her about Charlie and me. "Anytime."

"I'll call you tomorrow, Tyson," Tristan yells as he walks down the steps.

I close the door behind them and rub the back of my neck in frustration. Every time I try to talk to Zara, I'm interrupted. It's been three weeks, and she still doesn't know the truth. A scream interrupts my thoughts. I swing open the door, run down the steps, and onto my driveway. Zara is on the ground with her hand covering her nose. There's blood gushing out. "What did I tell you about talking back to me?" Tristan yells.

I push him out the way and rush to her side. "Zara, look at me."

She looks at me with a blood-stained face and tears in her eyes. All the anger I've been feeling washes over me. I stand and look for Tristan. Once I find him standing by the car, I stomp over to him and connect my fist with his jaw. He falls to the ground. "You want to hit someone, Tristan?" I kick him in his side. "Hit someone your own size."

"Tyson, what the hell?" Charlie appears in front of me. "What the hell is going on here?" Her eyes grow wide when she sees Zara.

Tristan staggers to his feet and puts pressure on his side. "You have nothing to do with this, Tyson. This is between me and my wife."

"That's where you're wrong. You're on my property, which means I have everything to do with it. Now, get the fuck out of here."

"Let's go, Zar," he says as he wipes blood from his lip.

I get in his face, up close and personal. "No. I said *you* go. Zara stays here."

"I'm not leaving here without my wife."

"He's right, Tyson, we shouldn't get involved," Charlie yells from behind me.

I ignore her. And keep my eyes on Tristan. "Unless you want me to break both your legs, I suggest you get in your car and leave."

He continues to stare me down. But he knows me. And he knows that I'm perfectly capable of doing exactly what I said I would do. He glances over at Zara, then back at me. "Fuck it. I don't feel like this shit tonight." He hops inside his car and speeds off. I walk back over to Zara and help her off the ground. "Are you okay?"

"Yeah, I'm sorry about all this."

"What? Zara, this isn't your fault."

Charlie doesn't bother helping us, and she doesn't seem to be concerned about what just happened to Zara. She folds her arms and narrows her eyes with jealousy. Zara takes notice. "Tyson, I don't want to cause any problems. I think I better call Tristan to come back."

"Good idea," Charlie replies.

"Stop it, Charlie."

"Don't you think we need to talk about this, Tyson?"

No. We don't need to talk about it because this is not up for discussion. But I grant Charlie her wish, out of respect. I turn to face Zara. "You're not leaving. Just give Charlie and me a minute to talk."

She glances between me and Charlie before she agrees. "Okay."

"Thank you. Please, go inside. You can take the guest bedroom. It's the fourth room on the right. Make yourself comfortable."

She nods before she turns around and walks toward the house. As soon as she's out of ears' reach, Charlie starts to yell. "What the hell were you thinking telling her she can stay here?"

"Can't you see she needs help? Or are you that selfish that you would rather see her leave with a man who beats her?"

"That man is her husband, and whatever their marital problems are, we have nothing to do with it. I'm leaving for a job in the morning, and I'm supposed to be okay with you having another woman staying in our home while I'm away?"

"I'm not turning my back on a friend."

"Oh, is that right? It seems to me you have no problem turning your back on Tristan."

"What's that supposed to mean?"

"It means that Tristan is supposed to be your friend, and now all of a sudden your loyalty lies with his wife?"

"As his friend, it's my job to let him know when he's fucking up. And right now, he's fucking up. He could have killed her, Charlie."

"You're not fooling anyone, Tyson. I see the way you look at her."

"Will you stop with the accusations?"

She shakes her head. "I'm not an idiot. I'll agree with tonight. Tomorrow morning, I want her gone."

"I can't promise you that. She's not leaving until I know she'll be safe."

She scoffs and shakes her head. Watching me with disgust before she stomps off and leaves me standing in the driveway. I follow suit and enter my home. I walk upstairs and look for her to continue our conversation. When I turn the knob to enter our bedroom, I find it locked. "Charlie, open the door."

She ignores me. I head down the hall to sleep in another bedroom, but not before I check on Zara. I find her sitting on the bed with an ice pack. "I hope you don't mind me borrowing this from the freezer."

"No not at all. How are you feeling"

"It's not as bad as it looks. Is Charlie okay? I heard you guys yelling."

"She'll be fine."

"Tyson, I can go home if me being here causes any problems. You two shouldn't be arguing while planning a wedding."

"You don't need to be concerned about that."

"Why not?"

"Because there won't be a wedding."

CHAPTER 11

ZARA

I'm confused and shocked. "What do you mean there won't be a wedding? She's wearing a ring."

He leans against the door. "When I met Charlie, I was at a point in my life where I felt like something was missing. We met, we dated, and naturally, for me, the next phase was marriage. I thought I would grow to love her. I thought time would make our connection stronger. But it hasn't."

"Why haven't you told her?"

"I don't want to hurt her. And quite honestly, I was okay with settling...until I met you. Zara, you make me feel more than what she's made me feel in the past year we've been together."

I shake my head. "Don't do this, Tyson."

He crosses the room. "I mean it."

I hold my hands out in front of me to stop him from coming any closer. "This house belongs to the both of you. And she's right down the hall. It isn't right to be saying these things to me here."

He shoves his hands in his pockets. "This is my house. It's in my name, and I paid for it." I fold my arms across my chest and cock my head to the side. "Okay. You're right. She lives here and has just as much say-so as I do. I'm sorry. I should show more respect for you and her."

"You need to be honest with her, Tyson."

"I know. And I will."

"Thank you for letting me stay."

"You're welcome. There're extra T-shirts in the drawer. Get some rest, and I'll see you in the morning."

He walks away, but I stop him when he reaches the door. "Tyson."

He turns around. "Yeah."

"You make me feel something too."

I roll over the next morning, almost forgetting where I am until I open my eyes. Tyson sleeps upright in the chair in the corner. Was he there all night? He couldn't have been. Not with Charlie right down the hall. He stirs before his eyes slowly open and land on me. "Good morning."

"Good morning. Were you here all night?"

He yawns. "No. I came in here after Charlie left this morning."

"She was okay leaving you alone with me?"

He chuckles. "Of course not, and there's a broken glass in the kitchen to prove it."

"I'm so sorry."

"Don't be." He watches me intensely. "Something's been bothering me all night."

"What?"

"Why do you stay?"

I don't expect him to get it. And I don't want to offer him a sob story. "Tyson, I don't..."

"Please Zara, I need to know. Why do you stay?"

His concerned eyes pierce mine, waiting for an answer. "I don't have a choice right now."

"You *always* have a choice."

"No. I don't"

"Why not."

I'm hesitant at first. But then I take a deep breath and tell him everything. Starting with how Tristan and I met. I tell him about my parents' plans for my future and how they didn't align with mine. I tell him the exact moment Tristan started hitting me. And lastly, I tell him my plan to get away. When I'm done speaking, his fists grip the armrests tightly. "You can't go back there."

I huff. "And where do you suggest I stay? Here?"

He shakes his head. "Let me figure something out."

"I have a plan. I don't need your help."

"Your plan is going to take too long. He could kill you before you get out of there."

"Tyson, stop. This isn't your problem, and this is why I didn't want to tell you. I don't need your pity."

He sits straighter in the chair. "Pity? Zara, I don't pity you. I want to help you."

"Thank you. But I can take care of myself."

"And how is that exactly? By sitting back and letting him use you as a punching bag?"

I grimace at his words. Because they hurt. He doesn't get it. "I just told you my story. About my parents. Do you think I *wanted* to live like this?"

"What about restraining orders, shelters?"

I scurry to my feet in anger. "A restraining order won't work if the damage is already done. Tell me, Tyson, how will a piece of paper help me if Tristan breaks into the house and kills me?

And you want to talk about shelters? I had a phone interview with an intake counselor once, and you know how it went?" My voice rises as I continue. "She treated me like another number on her list. I could hear the judgment in her voice. You think those people want to help women like me? Well, they don't. Most do it for the tax breaks and incentives."

When I'm done speaking, he rubs the back of his neck, unsure of what to say to me next. "Zara, I didn't mean to sound like I was judging you, because I'm not. It just isn't right what he's doing to you."

I fold my arms and ask the burning question in my mind. "Why do you care so much, Tyson? I mean, aren't you and Tristan friends?"

His eyes go cold. "We are *not* friends. We used to be."

"Then why continue talking to him? Why put up this act?"

"Because I need you close. I need you around to make sure you have help if you ever need it."

"So, you play nice with him to keep an eye on me?"

"Yes. Right now, it's the only way."

He rises from the chair. "I'll leave you to freshen up. I'll go clean up the mess Charlie made and start breakfast."

TYSON

It gave me comfort to watch her sleeping so peacefully this morning. I didn't sleep at all last night. My mind was spinning with ways to get her to leave Tristan and ways to break things off with Charlie. If I had any doubt about leaving her, that all flew out the window last night. She showed no sympathy regarding Zara's situation. She was ready to throw her to the wolves, all to ease her own jealousy. That's not the kind of woman I want to be with, let alone spend the rest of my life with. I almost said it when we argued this morning. She woke up and thought that I was going to send Zara back to Tristan. I tried to reason with her. I even asked what suggestions she might have to help Zara. And she offered none. The only suggestion she had was to send her home and stay out of her business. I told her she was heartless, and she smashed a glass on the floor before she walked out.

I turn around at the sound of footsteps. Zara enters the kitchen, dressed in fresh clothing, minus the white blouse she wore. She replaced it with one of my t-shirts. "Thanks for washing my clothes."

"You're welcome. Sorry I couldn't get the dirt stain out of your shirt."

"It's okay. Breakfast smells good."

I cooked pancakes, bacon, and eggs. "Thank you. Have a seat."

She sits at the table and watches me prepare her plate. "I'm going to call Tristan after breakfast."

I pour her a glass of apple juice, careful not to show how angry that statement makes me. "I don't think that's a good idea."

"I can't stay here, Tyson. You know that."

She could stay here, and there isn't a goddamn thing Charlie could do about it. But I would never put either of them in that type of situation. "Let me at least talk to him before you go back."

"Okay." She eats a forkful of her pancakes. "These are really good."

"Thank you."

"How did you learn to cook so well?"

"I enjoy it. It calms my nerves when I'm stressing out over a project."

"Any other surprise talents I need to know about?"

"Yeah, I'm good at gardening too. I planted those flowers in the front yard."

"Wow! You're just full of talents, huh?"

I take a seat next to her. "You don't know the half of it.

What about you? Any talent's you'd like to share?"

She thinks for a minute. "Outside of sketching? None that I can think of."

We smile at each other before she takes a sip of her juice. "What are you going to say to him?"

"I don't know yet. But I'm going to make it clear where he and I stand. I despise men who abuse women."

"Did you know someone who abused women?"

"Yeah. My father." She grows quiet. Surprised at my statement. "My father abused my mother."

Sympathy flashes in her eyes. "Tyson, I'm so sorry."

"For years I begged her to leave him. But she wouldn't listen. She told me to stay in a child's place. As I got older and stronger, I would intervene, and it would cause her and me to fight. I wanted to protect her, but no matter how hard I tried, she resisted."

"Did she ever leave him?"

Memories of that night shuffle out of order. "No."

"What happened?"

"He killed her."

Her fork drops as she gasps. "I'm sorry. I didn't know."

"It's fine."

"Did you call the police. Did he go to jail?"

"No. He died that night too."

"How?"

"I killed him."

Silence fills the room as she allows me to continue. "They had an argument. She was really going to leave him this time. She was going to take me, and we were going to go stay with my grandmother. He beat her badly. And when she fought back, he strangled her. I grabbed the knife from the kitchen and stabbed him in the back. But it was too late. He had killed her. I moved to New York with my aunt after that, God rest her soul."

"Tyson...I don't know what to say."

"That's why I care, Zara. That's why you can't go back there. I know firsthand what men like him do."

I need to protect her. I can't lose another person close to me at the hands of an abuser. And I can't sit in the background and do nothing about it. I listened to my mother. I tried to stay out of it. And look where that got her. Had I listened to my own instinct and tried harder to save her, she may still be alive. Her hand covers mine. "I don't want you worrying about me, Tyson. I will get out of this marriage safely. You have to trust me."

"I can't help but worry. Because I care about you."

She slides her hand back swiftly. "You can't."

"Why not?"

"Because my problems aren't your burden to carry."

"You're not a burden." She smiles at me warmly before sipping her juice. I stand to my feet. I'm suddenly not feeling myself, and I don't want to take anything out on her. "I'm going for a drive. Make yourself comfortable."

She looks around the kitchen. "Are you sure?"

I nod. "I'm sure. I'll be back in a little while."

She must sense my sudden change in mood because she doesn't resist. "Okay."

I grab my car keys and leave the house feeling unsettled. Talking about my mother stirred emotions in me I try hard to suppress. I can't let Zara see me this way. I need to let off some steam. I need to extinguish this burning fire growing inside of me. And I know just the way to do it. I start the car and head to Zara's house.

CHAPTER 12

ZARA

It feels strange being in Tyson's home alone. Hell, it feels strange being here at all. I started to leave this morning. I didn't want to cause any problems, regardless of Tyson's admission to me. But I must admit that I am afraid to go back. Tristan is getting worse. His abuse has always been hidden. To the outside world, he's a devoted, loving husband. But behind closed doors, he's anything but. Lately, he's been belittling me every chance he gets in front of Tyson. And became bolder last night when he struck me in his driveway. I had no idea I would set him off that way. The four of us were having a good night. I was relaxed, knowing Tyson was right across the table from me. At the end of the night, when we said our goodbyes, I offered to drive since Tristan had been drinking more. He declined. And I pushed the issue. That's when the scene unfolded in the driveway. He punched me for nagging him. How humiliating it was for Tyson and Charlie to witness me lying on the ground, helpless. I wanted to get up and run away. From everything and everyone. I was literally shaking when he helped me up off the ground.

My legs were weak, and so was my pride. Imagine my surprise when Tyson made Tristan leave without me. His demand for me to stay the night left me stunned, to say the least. From the beginning I wondered why he cared so much. Why he would choose to involve himself in such a complicated situation. It all made sense when he told me about his mother. How awful it must have been to witness his mother being hurt. I suddenly think about my situation. The idea of children crosses my mind. I tried to get pregnant after Tristan and I got married. But when the abuse started, I went on the pill. No way would I bring a child into an already toxic situation. I still want kids one day, if I'm lucky enough to remarry.

I grab a glass and pour myself some iced tea and head to the pool. I don't have a swimsuit, so I take my jeans off and lounge in the T-shirt. I cross my ankles and stare with appreciation at the oasis-style pool area. Pristine blue water, palm trees that look like the real thing, and a mini waterfall. I grab the fashion magazine next to me and flip through the pages. I shake my head at the images in front of me. Different designers, yet the styles look alike. Suddenly, an idea pops into my mind. I grab my phone and Google Tyson Wear. I scroll through the website and grow more and more excited as my idea takes form. I toss the magazine and hurry inside to search for a pencil and a notebook. I find both in a junk drawer in the kitchen. I rush to the nearest couch in an all-white room decorated with hints of gold. I plop down on the plush white couch and prop my feet up. My hands get to work. Image after image sears into my mind and comes to life on the paper in front of me. By the time I'm done, I've created three new items. I stare down at my work and smile. It's exactly what Tyson Wear needs. But will he like what I've done? Will he be okay with me taking his designs in a new direction? My eyes get heavy, and I decide to lie down for a nap, but not before scribbling *Tyson She-Wear* across the top of the paper.

TYSON

I've been sitting in my car for fifteen minutes now, debating if I've made the right decision by coming here. Confronting Tristan could make the situation worse, or it could make it better. And I seriously doubt it's the latter. I've tried to hold back for as long as I could, but I've reached my limit. I can't sit back and watch this happen any longer. I exit the car and ring the doorbell. The door swings open. "Where's Zara?" he asks.

"We need to talk. Can I come in?"

He thinks about it for a second before stepping to the side and allowing me to walk in. I follow him inside the kitchen, where I see he's on his third can of beer. "Unless you came to tell me you're bringing her home, we don't have shit to talk about."

"Zara is where she's safe."

"Safe from whom? Me?"

"Is that a serious question?"

He chuckles. "You don't know what the hell you're talking about. I'm only giving her what she deserves."

My forehead wrinkles in disgust. "You're hurting her. Since when did you start hitting women?

"What business is it of yours?"

"I hate everything about abuse toward women, including the men responsible for it."

He takes a long swig of his beer then slams the can on the counter. "Does Charlie know you're this concerned about Zara?"

"Just answer the question, Tristan."

He watches me for a second before his mouth slightly curves upward. "She gets out of line. She needs to be put in her place from time to time."

"Do you hear yourself right now? Out of line? Tristan, she's your wife."

"Right. She's *my* wife. And sometimes she forgets that she belongs to me, you know, kind of like how you forgot last night?"

"I didn't forget. I know she's your wife. But I also know you hit her. I came here to talk some sense into you before she comes home."

"I don't need you to tell me shit. And I don't appreciate you coming to my house trying to tell me how to treat her. I thought we were friends. You just met Zara, and you think it's your job to defend her? Why?"

Because you don't deserve her. I do.

It's like he can hear my thoughts. "Wait. Your attracted to her, aren't you?"

I wave off his comment. "It's not about that. It's about her safety, Tristan. You need help."

He laughs out loud. "Well, I'll be damned. I'm right. You're attracted to her."

"I won't stand around and let you hurt her."

"Well, you have no other choice now, do you?" He watches me with a smug look. "Big, bad Tyson. The man who has it all wants *my* wife. Well, guess what? You'll never have her."

I shake my head. "This was pointless. I tried to have a civilized conversation with you, but clearly this was a mistake. I'll leave, but just know that I'm not bringing her home until you get some help."

"We'll see about that."

"I'd like to see you try and stop me."

He grits his teeth. "Get the hell out of my house, Tyson."

I leave without saying another word. My instincts were right. This didn't go well, and I'm sure Zara will be handing in her resignation first chance Tuesday morning. I drive around the city for a while, allowing myself to cool off before I go home. I've made up my mind. I'm not letting her go back. I don't care how angry Charlie gets, or how much Zara fights me on it.

Her safety comes first, and right now, nothing else matters. Tristan thinks he has it all figured out. He guessed that I'm attracted to Zara, and I didn't deny it. Because it's common sense. Any man would be attracted to her. But he doesn't know how I feel about her. He doesn't know how thoughts of her fill every space in my mind. He doesn't know how much my body craves hers when we're away from each other. And he has no idea that I'll fight him to the death if it means protecting her.

The house is oddly quiet when I enter. I search each room until I find Zara stretched out on Charlie's seven-thousand-dollar couch. This room wasn't designed to be occupied. Charlie's sole intention was to make it look pretty and untouched. I never understood why—to me, it was a waste of money. But I let it go. I cross the room and stand over her. She sleeps peacefully with a notebook across her chest. I slide it from her hands gently and take another look at her before I open it. I stare in awe at the image in front of me. A curvy woman dressed in a navy-blue dress with a navy and pink scarf around her neck. The caption reads *Tyson She-Wear*. Her idea is golden, and I'm eager to see more. I lean down, kiss her softly on her cheek, and exit the room, carrying the notebook with me.

Zara walks into my bedroom about thirty minutes later, just as I flip the last page. Her eyes land on the notebook in my hand. "Figured I'd play around with some ideas."

"Come, sit next to me."

She sits beside me, and I open the notebook. "Zara, what were you thinking when you created these?"

She smiles as she swipes the book from me. "I was thinking that you don't offer any products for successful women. Seems a little sexist to me." I open my mouth to reply, but she laughs before I can answer her. "I'm just joking. But seriously, why do you only offer items for men?"

I shrug. "I guess women's clothing hasn't been a priority."

She shakes her head. "Well, it's time to change that. Women are just as successful as men."

"I agree. But I know nothing about women's fashion." I smile. "But you do." I point to the notebook. "Those are great ideas, Zara."

She blushes. "Thank you."

I stand. "I want to discuss something with you."

"Okay."

"I spoke to Tristan this morning."

"And?"

"It didn't go well."

"I knew that it wouldn't."

"He's lost his fucking mind, if you ask me."

"What did he say?"

"He said you forget who you belong to sometimes and that he has to put you in your place."

She giggles. "That sounds about right."

"Zara, this isn't a joke. Tristan has serious issues. I don't want you going back there."

She shoots to her feet. "We've been over this, Tyson."

"I know, but that was before he made it clear he won't get help."

She crosses her arms. "So, what do you suggest I do?"

"If I promise to keep my distance, would you stay here?"

"With you and Charlie?"

"I'm going to discuss it with her first. I'll make my position clear. Shit, you two can even share a room if you want, but at least I would know you were safe."

"Tyson, in what world do you think your fiancée would be okay with another woman moving in who isn't family?"

I place my arms on her shoulders. "Listen, I know it sounds crazy. And trust me, I don't want to put you and Charlie in a difficult situation. Despite me not wanting to marry her, I don't want to hurt her. I think we should all sit down and figure this out."

She throws her hands in the air. "Jesus, Tyson. Don't you understand? It won't work. Charlie loves you. There's no way she'll go for it. And even if she does…" She stops talking and faces me with tears in her eyes.

"Say it Zara."

She takes a deep breath. "Keeping our distance at work is one thing. But staying here, watching you with her, not being able to touch you or be near you, I…I won't be able to do it."

The exact same thing entered my mind. Being close to Zara and not being able to touch her is torture. Not to mention the fact that I need to have the conversation with Charlie about our relationship status. Zara shouldn't be here for that. I rub some of the stress out of the back of my neck, "I guess you're right. I'm not thinking clearly."

She shakes her head. "No. you aren't."

Zara went back to the guestroom, and I'm in my bedroom scrolling through some emails when the doorbell rings. I run down the steps to answer it. "What are you doing here?"

Tristan looks behind me. "I came to get, Zara."

I turn around, and Zara's walking down the stairs. When she reaches us, her face is filled with regret. "I called him."

"You what?"

How can she betray me like this? How can she go back to him so willingly after what he did to her? "Zara, please."

Tristan laughs. "You thought she'd leave me for you? She'll never leave me, Tyson. Not for you or anyone else."

Zara takes a step further, and I place my hand on her shoulder to stop her. "You don't have to do this."

Tristan shakes his head. "You look pathetic right now. Come on, Zar. Let's go home."

Her eyes meet mine, and I plead with her to stay. On one hand, I want to yank her behind me, beat the living shit out of

IN LOVE WITH HIS WIFE

Tristan, and slam the door in his face. But on the other hand, I know this is her choice. I need to let her make her own decision. She's about to make the same decision my mother made. She's choosing to stay. They all say they have a plan. They all say they will leave. But it rarely ever happens. "I'm sorry," she says softly."

CHAPTER 13

ZARA

I didn't want to hurt Tyson. And the look on his face right now is killing me. I had to call Tristan. I had no other choice. I don't belong here. He and I both know it. I'm standing in the middle, between him and Tristan, and I'm being pulled in each direction. I need to go home with my husband because Tyson doesn't deserve to be bothered by me and my marital problems. I need to fix my own issues and not be a burden to him. I need to set him free in a sense. "Zara..."

The sound of my name from his lips cracks my chest wide open. He's literally begging me not to go. I open my mouth to answer him, but Charlie appears from behind Tristan. Tristan laughs and moves out the way, allowing her inside. "Charlie, it's good to see you."

Tyson raises an eyebrow. "You're home early."

She glares at me. "Not early enough, I see."

The air is thick with tension and frustration. A minute ago, Tyson was begging me to stay, but now that Charlie is here, he looks unsure of what to do. His eyes swing between us. Charlie watches me with pure hatred. I need to get out of here. I place my hand on Tristan's arm. "Take me home, please."

Tristan smirks and leads me out the door. I turn around and look Tyson and Charlie in the eye. "I'm sorry for any problems I've caused."

Charlie shakes her head. "Just go."

I wait for Tyson to say something, but he doesn't. He curses to himself before turning around and stomping off. What have I done?

Tristan slams the refrigerator door. "You should have known better."

He opens the bottled water and takes a sip. "You're not working for him anymore."

I knew this was coming. It's what Tyson was trying to avoid. My plan is ruined. I'm out of a job and have nowhere near the amount of money I need saved to leave him. "Tristan, I'm not quitting."

He stiffens. "What did you just say to me?"

I change my tone. I become the begging, pitiful wife who asks for permission. "What happened won't happen again. I realized Tyson should have minded his own business."

He eyes me suspiciously. "Is that so?"

"Yes."

"He wants what's mine."

"No. He's in love with Charlie. He isn't interested in me."

"Oh, but I think he is, Zar. Why all the fuss over you?"

"He mentioned something about his mom dying from abuse."

A lightbulb goes off in his head. "That's right." He takes another gulp of water. "I forgot about what happened to his mother."

"See, it has nothing to do with me, Tristan. It was all about what happened to his mom. I told him I'll never leave and to stay out of it."

He doesn't look convinced. "I still don't like it."

"Please, Tristan. Please don't make me quit. I'll do anything."

He leans against the counter. "Anything?" He places the water bottle down. "Go upstairs and shower. Put on that outfit I like. The red one."

I nod.

"And hurry."

I shower quickly and step into the red silk strip of fabric that Tristan calls lingerie. I can't remember the exact time he got this for me. Maybe a birthday or an anniversary. I hear his footsteps grow closer as he climbs the steps. I wait patiently for him on the edge of the bed. He enters the room with a glass of vodka in his hand. He drinks the entire glass before placing it on the dresser. He watches me hungrily as he undresses. He tosses his clothes to the floor quickly then steps in front of me. "Get on your knees, Zar."

I don't want to. I don't want to put my mouth on him. But right now, I don't have a choice. I drop to my knees in front of him. He grabs a fistful of my hair and yanks my head back. "You've been defiant lately, and I think I should teach you a lesson. Would you like that?"

No.

"Yes."

He smirks as he removes his belt. He takes a step back, drops his jeans and boxers, then tosses his shirt. The roughness of the carpet burns through my knees, causing them to be sore. But I don't move. I wait patiently, just the way he likes. He steps out of his jeans and moves closer. He rubs his shaft in front of me, and the sight makes me sick to my stomach. I close my eyes. "Open your eyes, Zar, I want them on me."

I do as he says and open my eyes. He has the eyes of a

monster. Menacing. Cold. He grabs the back of my head. "Open," he demands.

I open my mouth slowly. He shoves it in forcefully, hitting the back of my throat. I find the will to prevent myself from gagging. He hates it when I do and tries to punish me for it. I wrap my lips around him, fighting the urge to bite down on him as hard as I can. The thought of him bending over in pain like I frequently do would be satisfying to watch. His grip on the back of my head tightens and moves it back and forth. I pretend to enjoy it as I suck him. Holding my breath to avoid the smell of him and slobbering as much as I can to drown out his taste. He stops suddenly. "Stop, that's enough."

I wipe the spit from my mouth and stand. I remove the lingerie, lie on the bed, and wait for him to join me. I pray that it's quick, so we can get this over with. He climbs on top of me and pushes roughly inside me. I'm not lubricated, and it hurts. He moves in and out forcefully, stretching me in the process. It stings. It feels like he's ripping me apart. But I keep it together for about five minutes before he collapses on top of me. He rolls over. "Damn. That was good this time."

"Yes, it was."

He's delusional. His idea of good and my idea of good are two different things. Good is how it feels with Tyson. I turn my head to the side, wishing it could be him lying next to me instead of Tristan. "I know you wonder why I changed. Why I became a different person than when we met."

I turn my head back to face him. "Yeah, I do."

He watches me for a few minutes before he turns on his back and stares up at the ceiling. "It's not that I don't love you, Zar. I wanted to be a good man, a good husband. But I guess it's true what they say. The apple doesn't fall far from the tree."

"What do you mean?"

I take a gamble by speaking. But I need to know. "I never

wanted to be like my father. He was a dick. He was mean. Treated my mother like shit."

I never knew much about Tristan's parents. He barely spoke about them, and when I asked, he said they had both died in a plane crash. He continues speaking. "I hated him for how he treated her. And I hated her for staying."

I want to probe further. Ask more questions to learn more about his upbringing. But I don't. If I push further, he'll become angry and shut down. He turns to face me. "So, you see, it's not my fault. I didn't marry you to treat you this way. I really wanted to be better, better than my father. But it's inevitable. His blood runs through my veins, and as much as I despise the man who made me, I'm just like him."

I'm saddened by his admission. Shocked by his willingness to open up about his parents, and I sympathize with him because I too watched my mother suffer abuse from my father. Hearing Tristan's story helps me understand his actions a little better. During my research into abusive partners, I learned that most men learn abusive behavior from someone close to them. It's like a cycle. Son watches dad abuse his mother, then in turns does the same to his partner. It's a revolving cycle until someone decides to change it. I suddenly don't feel sympathy anymore. Tristan has the power to be different. If he hates being this way so much, why not get the help to change? He must break the cycle, like what Tyson has done. My thoughts flash to Tyson's story. He watched his mother die at the hands of his father, yet he's not like his father at all. Or is he? I suddenly realize I don't know that much about his past to determine if he's being truthful. What if he has a pattern of abusing women as well? It's possible I may not have seen this side of him yet. "You're thinking I can change, aren't you?" he continues.

I nod. "You can do it, Tristan. You can see a therapist and get some help. You can be better."

He chuckles. "Who says I want to be better?"

"But you could be different. You can be..."

"No. I said I *wanted* to be different." He shrugs. "But I've finally accepted who I am."

Why did I bother? Why did I think I could get him to see reason? Did some small piece of me think that we could go back to the way things were? That he would suddenly become a different person overnight? I once loved Tristan. I used to care about his well-being, but not anymore. It's not my place anymore to make him see reason. It's none of my business if he wants to continue being the way he is. I need to think about myself. Do what's best for me until I'm able to leave. *If* I'm able to leave. After what's happened, I'm not so sure anymore. I told Tristan I would do anything to keep my job. I did what he asked. I came upstairs, dressed slutty, and submitted to his demands. So, what now? I clear my throat nervously, unsure if now is the right time to ask. "Um, is it okay if I still work for Tyson?"

He whips his head to the side. "I just shared something personal and difficult with you, and you're worried about working with him. He disrespected us, Zara. The answer is no. I don't want you anywhere near him."

Somehow, I knew that would be his answer. I knew deep down that he would forbid me to work with Tyson, even if I begged him. I say nothing. I act unaffected, even though I'm devastated. How will I get out of this now? Where will I go with little to no money and parents who won't let me come back home? He rises from the bed. "It's best you stay home anyway, with me running for governor. I'm announcing my bid soon, and I'll need you."

My breathing quickens. My heart tightens, and I feel hot. I feel like I'm having a panic attack. This can't be happening. I had a plan. He grabs his clothes off the floor. "I'm going to shower, and then I have someplace to be."

I cover myself with the blanket as he walks into the bathroom. I'm two seconds away from sobbing uncontrollably, but I manage to stay strong. I wanted to do this on my own. I wanted to stick to the plan and find my way out. But now it's impossible. I can't do it. I'm going to need help. Help from someone I trust. He's offered many times, and I've turned him down. I was too stubborn to realize he was right. That waiting too long will put me in danger. I won't take this abuse another day. Tomorrow, I'll find a way out of this house and go straight to Tyson. And hopefully, he'll still help me.

TYSON

As soon as Zara left with Tristan, my house turned into World War III. Charlie stormed into the sitting room where I was seated on the couch, taking a shot of tequila. *Angry* isn't the word to describe her. She was like a typhoon. Screaming and throwing her hands in the air. "How long were you going to let her stay here?"

"Is that why you came back so early, to spy on me?"

"I'm not explaining why I decided to come home early to *our* home."

I stand and grab the tequila bottle from the bar. I take a swig directly from it. "I don't have the time or the patience for this right now."

"The hell you don't. You don't have the time to have a discussion with me, but you took all the time in the world to help her?"

"How many damn times do I have to tell you that I wasn't going to sit back and allow him to beat her?"

"Tyson, you're my fiancé. I should be your only concern. Me and our wedding."

"There's not going to be a wedding, Charlie."

I release a deep breath after I say it. The weight of it finally lifting off me. The room remains quiet. She shakes her head. "What are you saying?"

"I'm saying that I rushed into this. I shouldn't have proposed."

"You...you don't mean that, Tyson."

I want to punch myself for hurting her. I want to blink and unsee the tears sliding down her cheeks. "Shit, Charlie, I..." I can't finish my sentence because I don't know what to say. I feel sorry for doing this, but I needed to tell her the truth. "Charlie, I'm sorry."

She wipes a tear then gains her composure. "You're serious? You want to call off the wedding?"

"Can you honestly say that we love each other?"

"I care deeply for you, Tyson."

I place my glass down. "And that's what you want to base our marriage on? You want our vows to say that we promise to deeply care for each other for the rest of our lives?"

"People can grow to love each other."

I take a step toward her. "I'm not taking that chance. I'm not marrying someone hoping that one day I *might* love her."

She crosses her arms. "Fuck you, Tyson. Things were going well before you allowed that bitch to make a mess of things. You didn't care too much about being in love before then."

"You're being disrespectful, and you're better than that. Zara has nothing to do with my decision. I felt this way long before I met her."

The sound of her slapping me echoes in the room. I place my hand on my burning cheek and take a step back just in case she's met with the desire to hit me again. "I guess I deserved that."

"I could have had any man I wanted, Tyson. I've rubbed elbows with powerful men all my life. Some more powerful than you. But I *chose* to be with you. I thought we would make the perfect team."

"Charlie—"

She holds a hand up to stop me from speaking. "No. I don't

want to hear it. I know what this is really about. You have feelings for her."

I shake my head. "No, I..."

I stop myself from speaking another lie. Charlie deserves to hear the truth, regardless of how it will make her feel. I've spent a year with this woman. I should have enough respect to be honest with her. "Yeah, I do."

"Did you sleep with her?"

I nod.

She laughs out loud. "And you think she'll leave her husband for you?"

"I'm not asking her to. I'm not breaking things off with you to be with Zara. Like I said, she has nothing to do with my decision."

"She has everything to do with it!" she yells.

I reach out to touch her. To calm her. But she jerks away from me. "Don't touch me."

"Charlie, I'm sorry. I never meant to hurt you."

"Well, I guess it's over, then. I'm leaving. And don't call me when you realize she'd rather stay with her husband than be with you."

CHAPTER 14

ZARA

Tristan came home late and slept like a baby. I got up early and snuck out of the house. I'm going to ask Tyson for help this morning. But not in the sense that he may think. I need him to give me a loan, help me leave the state. I'll promise to pay him back as soon as I can, even if I sign a promissory note. I knock on his office door hoping he's here. The door swings open. He doesn't say anything. He takes a step back and allows me in. When the door shuts, he stands in place. "I'm surprised you're here."

"I don't have much time."

My eyes travel down his body. Now is not the time to be lusting over him, but I just can't help myself. His white-collared shirt is fully opened, revealing his chest. I suddenly have flashbacks of his hands gripping me. Visions of him telling me to come. Gosh, why does he have to be so sexy? He walks past me and stops in front of his desk. He starts to button his shirt. "I spilled coffee on my other shirt. I just changed it before you showed up."

I avert my eyes. "I need to talk to you."

"And I need to talk to you. After everything we discussed, why would you leave with him?"

"I thought it was for the best. I didn't want to intrude."

"You know that wasn't the case. I tried calling you. Texting you. You didn't respond. Do you have any idea how worried I've been? I almost sent a police car to your house to do a welfare check."

"I'm okay. Tristan hid my iPhone and laptop."

"He'd better return it. That's company property." He closes the gap between us and searches my eyes. "Did he hurt you?"

"No. But he's not letting me work for you anymore."

What happened between Tristan and me last night is not something I choose to discuss with Tyson. It's embarrassing and demeaning. It's bad enough he's witnessed firsthand how Tristan treats me. What would he think if he knew Tristan had me on my knees and fucked me like an escort? He walks around to his desk and opens a drawer. He pulls a notebook out and hands it over to me. "I wanted to give this back to you."

I take the notebook and run my fingers across the front, watching my dreams of working with Tyson vanish. Tyson rounds his desk and pulls me toward him. "You don't need Tristan to *let* you do anything. Besides, I was going to fire you anyway."

My heart drops. "What?"

"I was going to fire you because I don't need you working for me anymore. I need you working beside me."

"I don't understand."

He taps the notebook in my hands. "These designs. They're just what Tyson Wear needs. But I don't want the responsibility of building a woman's line. I want you to do it. Zara, I'm asking you to join me as a partner."

"Me?" I ask.

"Yes, Zara. You."

"Tyson, I don't know what to say."

"Say you'll join me."

I can feel the look of uncertainty settle on my face. The indecisiveness. Finally, I smile and release a breath of air. "Okay. I'll do it."

He leans in and kisses me. The kiss is enough to bring me to my knees. I pull away and look up at him. "I came here to finally accept your help. I was going to ask you for a loan. To help me flee the state, hell, even the country."

He watches me seriously. Like the thought of me leaving him cripples him with fear. "I'm not letting you run away, Zara. But I will help you. You'll be helping me run my company now. You'll have more than enough money to support yourself. With your salary, along with stock options and generous bonuses, you'll be set. And you never have to go back to that house. I have a place where you can stay."

I shake my head. "You know I can't stay with you and Charlie."

"I broke things off with Charlie last night. She's gone."

My eyes widen in surprise. "Oh."

"But I wasn't talking about my house. I mean, you're always welcome, but I have a place you can stay where you'll be a bit more comfortable. A place where Tristan can't find you."

He releases me from his embrace and grabs a brochure from his desk. He hands it to me. "It's all ready for you to move in."

I open the brochure. It's a private community with a golf course, tennis court, pool, and gym. When I read further, I'm taken aback by the layout of the apartments. They're fully furnished. The rooms are spacious, and everything looks brand new. "What is this place?"

"It's an apartment building I invested in. I own them. You can stay there until we figure out what to do about Tristan."

"We?"

"Yeah, we. I'm in this with you, Zara."

I flip another page. "This is a lot, Tyson. Can I think about it?"

It's a lot to think about. The offer to become his partner. The apartment. I don't want to agree so hastily. "Sure. But would you like to see it in person to help with your decision?"

"Yeah. But I can't be gone too long. I left a note telling him I've gone grocery shopping."

"Okay. Let's go."

We arrive at the gated community, where Tyson flashes a card that allows security to let him through. We pull around and enter a garage. "You'll be assigned your own spot."

Once he's parked the car, he exits and opens my door for me. We take the elevator up to the seventh floor. Once we've reach the door, he hands me the key. I unlock it and walk inside. The open floorplan allows for perfect lighting. The furniture is contemporary yet modern. "Take a tour. I need to make a call."

He walks away with his phone to his ear, and I step inside the kitchen. My hand slides along the granite countertops and white cabinets. I walk further down the hall and enter the bedroom. The king-sized bed is decorated with black sheets and a black comforter. It's dark but sensual. "Do you like it?"

I whirl around to find Tyson standing in the doorway. "It's beautiful."

He steps inside the room and looks around. "You'll be safe here." He wraps his arms around my waist. "This place will be yours, Zara. You won't have to worry about me popping in unannounced just because I own the place. I'll only come over if you want me to."

I wrap my arms around him. "Thank you. I..."

I don't get to finish my sentence because my phone rings. I look at the caller and then at Tyson. "It's Tristan."

"Answer it."

I accept the call. "Hello."

"Where are you?"

"I'm running errands."

"Running errands where?"

"I went grocery shopping, and now I'm at the supply store looking for new pencils and markers."

"You ran out of those already?"

"Yeah, I used my last colored pencil yesterday."

"Okay. Well, next time check with me *before* you leave the house."

"Sorry. Okay."

"I'll see you at home."

"Yeah, see you at home."

I end the call. Tyson's staring at me, waiting for an update. "Everything okay?"

"Yeah, everything's fine."

"Good. Because I'm in no rush to let you go."

He kisses my neck tenderly. My skin sizzles at his touch. I reach for the buttons of his shirt and unbutton each of them quickly. When his shirt opens, I swiftly shove it off him. My hands roam his chest, gliding over every single muscle. He pulls me in tighter and places his mouth at my ear. "You have no idea how much I've missed you."

I'm eager. Ready for Tyson to strip me bare and make love to me. I've missed him too. I've missed his touch. He slowly undresses me until I'm left wearing nothing. The room is quiet except for the sound of my heartbeat. Seeing him watch me with lust-filled eyes makes me weak in my knees. He shoves his shirt off and kisses me again. I pull him closer to me, wrapping my arms around his neck and walking backwards toward the bed. When my legs hit the foot of it, I stop and pull my lips away from his. "You're still dressed."

He smirks before he takes a step back. "Then let's change

that."

My eyes sparkle with anticipation as I watch him remove his belt. Desire devours me as I watch him toss his clothing to the floor piece by piece. He places his finger under my chin and raises it. "Better?"

"Much better."

My patience has faltered. I no longer have the strength or resistance to wait for him to touch me. I throw myself at him. Kissing him. Touching him. We fall onto the bed with him between my legs. I pull my lips away from his. "I can't wait any longer, Tyson, I need you."

He hooks an arm around my leg and lifts it. He watches me with hooded eyes as he enters me. I feel nothing but pure pleasure as he strokes me with intensity. I meet him thrust for thrust, begging for all of him. "You're mine, Zara. I don't give a damn who says otherwise."

"Yes."

"Say it."

"I'm yours."

His tongue slides into my mouth as he kisses me. His strokes go deeper and deeper. "Give it to me, baby."

I scream his name as I come, holding him tightly while he does the same. And when we're finished, I know I can never go back to the way things were.

He smiles at me before he positions himself on his side. He props himself up with an elbow. "You okay?"

"Never better."

"Will you stay here?"

I exhale loudly. "Yeah, I will."

"Yeah?"

"Yep. I'll stay here."

He moves to kiss me, but I stop him. "But I have to do this strategically."

"What do you mean?"

"Tristan's being honored tonight for his work with the police force. I have to be there."

"You don't have to be there. There's no need for you to support him if you're leaving him."

"I'll be okay. I'll go home, and we'll go to the event together tonight. He's going to drink. And once we get back, he'll pass out. I'll grab some things and meet you."

"Some things? Zara, I can get you everything you need?"

"Not my designs. It's my work, and I need them."

This seems to make him understand. He nods. "Then I'll go with you. I'll tell him about us. You know I won't let him get anywhere near you."

I shake my head. "No. It's better if I grab my stuff and sneak out. Tristan is well connected, and I don't want the risk of him calling the cops or making a scene."

"I don't give a damn about him calling the cops. My legal team can take all their badges at the drop of a dime. I don't like this plan of yours, Zara."

"Please, Tyson. Trust me on this. It's better this way. Okay?"

He looks reluctant, but he fights the urge to disagree with me again. "Okay."

I smile as I work the room with Tristan. But unlike all the other times, my smile is genuine. I'm happy. I'm excited. Because tonight will be the last time I'll ever have my arm looped through his. "You're in a good mood," he says as he reaches for his third drink tonight.

I smile widely. "This is a big deal for you, Tristan. I'm proud of you."

He takes a sip of his scotch. "Yeah, it is, isn't it?"

"Yup."

"Damn, I'll be announcing my bid for governor in a few

weeks. I did it, Zar."

"Yes, you did."

He kisses me on the cheek. "Things are going to change for us. In a good way. I promise you."

I nod. *I won't be around to find out.*

I'm about to take a sip of my wine when a familiar face approaches us. It's the same blonde who was hanging on his arm at the Mayor's Ball. "Tristan."

He looks shocked. Caught off Guard. "Cicely. I didn't think you would be here."

Her eyes meet mine. "Of course. I couldn't miss your big night, now could I?"

She extends her hand to me. "I don't think we've met before. I'm Cicely."

I place my hand inside of hers. "I'm Zara."

"Tristan's wife, right? It's nice to finally meet you."

"Thank you. And you are?"

"Oh, I'm sorry. Tristan and I worked closely on his last campaign. We became good friends, isn't that right, Tristan?"

I should slap her. And not because she's hinting at the fact that she's fucked my husband. But because she's an idiot. She thinks she has the prize. That she should get some reward for sneaking around with him behind my back. Well, I've got news for her. Honey, you can have him. And all that comes with him. Tristan answers her question. "I wouldn't call us good friends, but you were a pleasure to work with."

I wish I could take a snapshot of her expression right now. Anger settles on her face. Silly girl. Tristan isn't who you think he is, and if you stick around long enough, you'll find out.

The night is almost over, and I make a quick run to the lady's room. Tristan is drunk, just like I knew he would be. As soon as we get home, he'll pass out and I can grab my stuff and run. A stall door swings open, and out walks Cicely. I ignore her as I wash my hands. She turns the water on at the faucet next to me and watches me through the mirror. "Zara, right?"

I turn the faucet off and grab a paper towel. "You know my name, Cicely."

She smiles. "Tristan barely talks about you. I didn't know he had a wife until a few months ago."

I shrug. "Well, now you know."

I walk past her, eager to get out of here. I'm not wasting my time being catty over a man I'm hell bent on leaving. "He doesn't love you, you know."

I stop in my tracks and turn around. "Excuse me?"

"I said he doesn't love you. He loves me. And he's loved me for the past year now. He's going to leave you as soon as he wins the race for governor."

I stare at her for two long seconds before I burst out with laughter. This angers her. "What the hell is so funny?"

I shake my head. "Good luck, Cicely. You're going to need it."

Tristan was quiet on the drive home. Maybe because he was too drunk to speak. When we enter our home, he heads straight to the kitchen for a beer. He pops the can open just as my foot lands on the first step. "Wait, I want to talk to you."

I take a deep breath and walk inside the kitchen. "Okay."

"Don't worry about Cicely. She's a flirt, but I can assure you there's nothing going on between us."

Liar.

"Okay."

He nods to the kitchen table. "Have a seat."

. . .

"Can I change out of this dress first?"

"No. I need you to answer some questions."

"Questions about what?"

"Questions like where you were this afternoon."

"I already told you. I was running errands."

He places the beer down on the counter. "Did running errands include stopping to see Tyson?"

How does he know?

"I—"

"I told you I didn't want you anywhere near him."

"I know, but—"

"Shut up!" he yells. He takes a few steps toward the table. "Did you think I wouldn't find out?"

He steps closer. "That pretty little thing that works for Tyson. She'll do anything for a few thousand dollars."

"Pam?"

"Yeah. Pam."

"When I woke up this morning and saw you were gone, I drove straight to Tyson's office. I had a feeling you would defy me and see him anyway. When I got there, Pam said I had just missed him. I asked if he left alone. At first, she wouldn't tell me. But once I gave her the money, she told me you were there this morning. And that the two of you left together."

"Tristan—"

In the blink of an eye, he punches me with a force so strong, it knocks me out of my chair and to the floor. My ears are ringing, and my face feels like it's on fire. He stands over me. "You lied to me." He kicks me in my ribs with his hard shoes.

"Please," I beg.

The next kick lands on my face. "Shut up, you lying bitch."

I touch my face and whimper as the blood coats my fingertips. I gasp for air as I try to crawl toward the stairwell. He laughs at my attempts. "Oh, you think you can run from me?" The tip of his shoe is the last thing I see before I black out.

CHAPTER 15

TYSON

Zara isn't answering my phone calls or my texts. And I'm starting to worry. Could she have changed her mind? No, she couldn't have. I look down at the messages I've sent.

Me: Just arrived. See you when you get here.

Me: Where are you? You're late.

Me: Are you okay? I'm getting worried.

Me: If you don't answer me, I'll drive over there and get you myself.

She's answered none of my messages, and her phone is going straight to her voicemail. I don't understand it. We had a well-thought-out plan. I did this her way. And she stood me up. I tap my fingers on the kitchen table as I debate driving to her house. It's killing me wondering where she is, but I don't want to pop up and ruin things just in case her plan is delayed for whatever reason. I'm at the apartment. The apartment she'll be living in. I came here just in case she decides to show up. We were supposed to meet at the bar around the corner from her house. Someplace close where she could run to and crowded with people in case Tristan followed her. She'd hop in my car, and I'd bring her here. I waited for her until the bar closed, but she never showed up. Now it's the morning and still nothing. I grab my phone and dial Pam.

"Hey, you're not in today?"

"Something came up. Has Zara called, been by the office this morning?"

"No. I haven't seen her since she left with you yesterday."

"Okay."

"Is everything alright?"

"I don't know. I can't reach her, and I think she might be in trouble."

There's a moment of silence. "Her husband stopped by this afternoon."

I straighten my spine. "What did he want?"

She takes a deep breath. "He asked if I had seen Zara."

"What did you tell him?"

She doesn't answer. "Pam, what did you tell him?"

"Okay. I didn't tell him anything at first. But then he offered me two thousand dollars, and I told him she left with you. I didn't think it was a big deal since she works here."

I spring to my feet. "Fuck!"

"Did I do something wrong?"

"Yes, you did something *very* wrong. And you're fired."

I end the call, grab my car keys, and race out of the house.

Twenty minutes later, I'm in her driveway. I slam my car door shut and bang on the front door. No one answers. I bang again. And again. I knock for at least fifteen minutes before I give up and walk back to my car. I take my phone out and call her. It goes to her voicemail again. I want to kick the door down. Smash in all the windows. The thought of her being inside and needing help makes me feel hopeless. I dial Tristan's number and get his voicemail as well.

"Fuck!" I yell.

I can't take this. I'm going to find out where she is one way or another. I drive across town to see the one person I know who can help me. Justin. I walk past his receptionist, who tries to stop me, and right into Justin's office without knocking. His eyes grow wide when he sees me. He says a few more words before he ends his call. I tell him everything. About Charlie. Zara and me. And what Tristan does to her. "It won't matter if she doesn't press charges."

"He's hurt her. I can feel it. Can't we send the cops there to arrest him?"

"Yeah, we can send the cops there. But if she denies it, and from what you've told me, she has a history of denying his abuse, there's nothing the cops can do."

I slam my fist on the desk. "Dammit, Justin. I can't wait around for her to end up in a fucking hospital or six feet under. There has to be something we can do."

He places his hand on my shoulder. "Hey, calm down."

"I can't calm down right now. Not until I know she's okay."

"You love this woman."

I hang my head. "Yeah, I do"

He pats my back. "I'll make a few calls."

ZARA

My eyes flutter, but my right eye won't open all the way. I try to force it open, but the pain is too much to bear. The pressure weighs heavily around my mouth from the swelling. I turn my head slowly and look at the clock. It's ten a.m. "Glad you're up."

Tristan sits on the edge of the bed next to me. "I called Dr. Newton. He said to put some ice on the swelling and for you to get plenty of rest."

Dr. Newton is our family doctor. He's never once done a house call, which means Tristan most likely paid him or offered him some kind of perk once he's governor. He smiles at me like the sick bastard he is. "You'll be okay, Zar." A tear slides down my cheek. "Hey, don't cry. If you're in pain, I have some pills for you. Just tap your finger once if you want them."

I'm in excruciating pain, but I do nothing. He grabs the prescription bottle and takes out a small pill. "You're so fucking stubborn. Here, take the damn pill. No need lying there in pain." I don't take it. "Take the fucking pill, Zar."

I open my hand, and he drops the pill inside. I pop it in my mouth and slip it under my tongue when he turns to reach for the glass of water. When he hands it to me, I drink it, then I return the glass to him. He smiles before he stands. "That pill is going to make you sleep for hours. I have something I need to take care of, but I'll be back. I'll wake you up so you can eat dinner, okay?"

I nod.

"You know I love you, right?"

Fuck you.

I nod.

"Good. I'll see you in a few hours."

He walks away but stops when he reaches the door. "I took your phone since you can't be trusted." I spit the pill out as soon as he leaves the room. The tears burn my cheeks as they slide down rapidly. I'm beaten. Broken. Sore. But I've got to find the strength to get out of here when he leaves. Because it may be my only chance.

I open the door and climb out of the cab. "Are you sure you don't want to wait? I can get you the money."

She shakes her head with tears in her eyes. "I've seen this type of thing happen before, Miss. Happy to help any way I can. This one's on me. Just stay safe, okay?"

I choke back the tears as I nod. "Okay. Thank you."

I watch her pull away then limp toward the security station. The guard steps outside the booth. "Miss, are you okay?"

"I'm Zara. Zara Price. I was here yesterday with Mr. Reed."

"Yes, I know who you are, Mrs. Price. Mr. Reed said to call him if you showed up here."

Relief sweeps through me as I release a huge breath of air. "Here, have a seat." He guides me to the chair inside the booth and sits me down slowly. He takes his phone out and dials a number. Tyson picks up, and they exchange a few words. When he hangs up, he steps close to me. Pity is written all over his face. "Mr. Reed has instructed me not to leave your side."

"Would it be okay for me to wait inside the apartment?"

"No, ma'am. I have strict orders to guard you like my life depends on it. Mr. Reed will be here soon."

I don't know how fast Tyson was driving, but his car speeds into the development and skids when he comes to a stop. He hops out of the car and runs toward the booth. "Zara. Jesus..."

I can't do this here. Not in front of the security guard. "Not here, Tyson. Just take me inside, please."

He looks at the security guard. "Thank you, Leon."

"No problem, boss."

He picks me up and carries me to the car. I'm sobbing in his arms before he even opens the door. I'm crying for all of it. The embarrassment. The shame. The physical pain. The relief of running away from Tristan. He places me inside and wipes my tears. "Shh, baby, don't cry. You're safe now."

"I'll fucking kill him." Tyson paces back and forth near the living room window. "I'm serious, Zara. I'll break his fucking neck."

I place my glass of warm apple cider on the coffee table. "It's over now, Tyson. I'm never going back."

"Goddamn right you're never going back. He needs to pay for what he did. Look at your fucking face."

I lower my head in shame at his statement. He's right. My face is a mess. I look like something out of a horror movie. He takes a seat next to me. "Zara." I raise my head to look at him. "I hate that he did this to you."

"I know."

"What happened?"

"He came to find me at the office. Pam told him we left together. After the party, he snapped and...did this." I point to my face. "He beat me so bad that he had to call our doctor to come to the house and examine me."

"And he didn't report it? He let Tristan get away with it?"

"Yeah. He did. I told you Tristan is connected. Do you know how many of his colleagues and friends have seen my bruises? They've never said anything, and they never will."

He places his hand on top of mine. "How did you get out?"

"He gave me a pill that he said would put me to sleep, but I didn't swallow it. As soon as he left the house, I got dressed, called a cab, and came here. I still had the brochure in my purse."

He shakes his head. "I've been going crazy. I didn't know what happened to you. If you hadn't called me today, I was going to storm in there like a SWAT team."

I cock my head to the side. "Are you serious?"

He smiles. "As a heart attack. I had plans to bust windows and break down doors to find you."

"You would have been arrested."

He stands to his feet. "And I wouldn't have cared. Come on, let's get you cleaned up."

I'm lying in bed, wearing one of Tyson's T-shirts. He ran me a nice, hot bath and then made me a sandwich. He put an ice pack on my swelling and gave me a few pills to help with my pain. He sits in the chair across from the bed now and scrolls through his phone. His face is tight. "Are you okay?"

He pauses and looks up. "Someone hurt the woman I love. No. I'm not okay."

My breath hitches. Did he just say that he loves me? He types something on his screen and stands. "I'm going to see Tristan."

I shake my head. "No. Let it go. I'll tell him I'm leaving. That I want a divorce."

"And you think he'll let you walk away just like that?"

"Yeah."

"Zara. Men like Tristan won't let you walk away. Especially with him being a politician. He has too much to lose."

"So, what should I do?"

"*You* will do nothing. Let me handle this."

"Handle it how?"

He hands me his phone. "Take a look."

I read the email. And if my face weren't swollen, I'm sure my eyes would be as wide as saucers. "What is this?"

"That is how we get Tristan to walk away peacefully. I hired a private detective. Tristan's been embezzling campaign money. Bribing officials. And…" He stops for a second. "He's having an affair."

"I know," I reply as I continue reading the information. "I've known for a while."

"But did you know that she's pregnant?"

I stop and look up at him. "No. I didn't"

"Think about it. There's no way he'll want this information to leak. It'll ruin any chance of him becoming governor and strip him of every award he's ever won as mayor."

A smile spreads across my swollen face. "I'll finally be free."

"I've dreamt about the night I get to hold you."

I trail my fingers on his arm. "Me too."

"Zara. I need to say something."

"Okay."

"I knew Tristan was mistreating you from the first time I laid eyes on you. I've been patient. I've held back like you asked, lingered in the background, doing nothing while he mistreated you. It stops today. He'll *never* hurt you again."

His body stiffens when he says it. I can feel the anger rolling off him. I turn my head to the side. "I love you too."

The words blurt out on their own accord, but I mean them. I love him. I don't know when it happened, but I do. He leans in close and places his lips on mine carefully. I grab his hand and place it on my breast. His eyes bore into mine. "As much as I'd like to have you scream my name right now, you need to rest."

"I'm okay."

He smirks as he lightly squeezes it. "Your body needs to relax, sweetheart, and your mind does too."

I swat his hand away. "You're such a tease."

He leans in and kisses my neck. "Do you miss me touching you, baby?"

"Yes."

His hand moves between my legs and under the T-shirt I'm wearing. I'm not wearing any panties, making it easy for him to reach me. "Open your legs," he says into my ear.

I open my legs wider as the wetness collects in my most sensitive spot. He moves his fingers and slowly rubs my folds. "Oh..."

"Is this what you want?"

"Yes, more, please."

My eyes roll to the back of my head as he circles my clit. He's lying beside me, speaking lustfully into my ear. "Relax. Let Go. Let me please you. Let me take care of you."

"Mm hmm."

He inserts a finger. "Fuck, that feels good." He kisses my neck again as his finger goes deeper. "Tyson."

"That's right. Tell me what you need."

"I need..."

"Tell me."

"Oh, God..."

"Let it go. Let it go, baby."

My body shivers as I come with his finger still inside me. I cry out as the orgasm ripples through my body. His finger lingers inside me as I clinch around it. When I'm finished, he pulls it out gently. "Feel better?"

I smile in satisfaction. "Much better. But what about you?"

"I can wait. Tonight was about pleasing you. Giving you a release so you can relax."

I've never met a man so selfless. And I'm not just talking about the sex. Tyson's goal has always been to protect me. To keep me safe. No matter what. He didn't care about how it would affect his friendship with Tristan. He did what was right, even though his fiancée at the time didn't like it. There could be a happy future for us, or maybe not. But whatever happens, I'll always be grateful for him. "What are you thinking about?"

His voice pulls me out of my thoughts. "You."

"What about me?"

"I know I didn't make it easy for you when you first offered me help. But I'm glad that you did. Thank you, Tyson. Thank you for—"

"Shh." He places a finger against my lips. The scent of me coating it. "Marry me."

I rise up quickly. "What?"

"Marry me, Zara."

"But I'm already married."

"My lawyer has already drafted divorce papers. All you need to do is sign them."

Is this what I want? Is *he* what I want? The answer comes immediately: yes. I want to be with Tyson. But a small piece of me is scared to jump from one person to another. A part of me still craves to find my own way. "Tyson, I can't jump right into another marriage."

"You don't have to. Take all the time you need, Zara. Two days. Two weeks. Two years. I don't care. Just promise me that once you're ready, you'll be mine."

"You'll...wait for me?"

He nods. "You're everything I've been searching for. Everything I've ever wanted. Now, I know you want to do things your way. Gain your independence back. Take the time to heal from…" He pauses and takes a deep breath. "To heal from everything you've been through. I'll help you through it, and if you don't want my help, I'll be there in case you fall. I'll always protect you, baby. I'll always take care of you. Just let me love you."

My chest grows heavy, and my nose sniffles as the tears form. "Yes."

He pulls me into a hug. "You've made me a very happy man."

When he releases me, my smile disappears as a question forms in my head. "I hate to spoil the moment, but what if Tristan refuses to sign the divorce papers?"

"He'll sign them. Or I'll make sure all his dirt is front page news."

"But what if he still refuses? What if he refuses to let me go?"

Panic settles in my chest. Fear creeps down my spine. He takes my hands in his. "Let me worry about Tristan."

I want to let it go and allow him to handle it. But my gut doesn't trust it. I feel like it's a bad idea to let Tyson try to blackmail Tristan. It could be that I'm just being paranoid. Suffering from abuse can cause you to be fearful and nervous all the time. But I don't have to be that way anymore. I have someone who'll protect me. If I'm ever going to have a peaceful life, I'll have to let him do this. "You're right, Tyson. I'll let you take care of it."

CHAPTER 16

TYSON

I'm up early the next morning on a mission. I left Zara a note and had breakfast delivered until we can go grocery shopping. I hadn't intended on asking her to marry me. Not right away anyway. She's been through a lot. And I know she needs time to heal. I knew one day I would make her mine, but when she was ready. But I couldn't help it. I kept telling myself to give it a few years. That it would be better to wait and see what our relationship blooms into. But as much as I wanted to wait, something was nagging at my soul to ask her right then and there. So, I did. I followed my instinct and asked her to be my wife. And she said yes. I don't know when we'll get married. I haven't even taken the time to buy her a ring. But all that matters to me right now is that she said yes. I enter Justin's office. "Good to see you again. I didn't think you'd be here so quickly."

"I didn't want to waste any time. Are the documents ready?"

He grabs a stack of papers. "Yes, here they are."

I flip the page and read the first paragraph. "And what happens if he doesn't sign these?"

"If he doesn't sign the papers willingly, then a hearing will proceed. Zara will have to explain to the judge her reasoning for filing."

"Other than him beating her?"

"*Allegedly* beating her."

"I saw her fucking face, Justin."

He raises his hands in surrender. "Hey, you know I believe you. But without any evidence or witnesses, it'll be hard to convince the judge."

"What about the doctor? He was at her house to take care of her. He saw what Tristan did."

"You said yourself he's being paid under the table. The likelihood of him turning on Tristan is slim to none."

I ball my fist. "I should beat it out of him myself."

Justin crosses his arms. "I know this isn't what you want to hear, Tyson. But it's how the system works."

"He deserves to rot in prison for what he's done."

"I agree. But there are steps that need to be taken to get him there. Right now, the odds are not in our favor."

"What about the information I sent you? Can't we use that to speed the process along?"

He looks behind me, then he leans in and speaks in a low voice. "You're asking me to put my job on the line by bribing him."

"No. I'm not asking you to do it. But what if I do? What if I give the information I have to the police?"

"You got that information illegally, Tyson. It most likely won't hold up in court."

"So, what do we do, then? It seems like we're damned if we do and damned if we don't. I promised to protect her, and I *will* keep that promise. No matter what I have to do to keep it."

"Let me do my job. Trust me on this. I'll get the papers signed, a full restraining order, spousal support…"

"No spousal support. She doesn't need a dime from him. Just get the papers signed as quickly as you can."

I continue to read through the documents carefully before signing in each spot. "Are you sure about this, Tyson?"

"I'm sure," I reply as I sign the last page and shove the papers toward him. "Are we all set?"

He checks each page before answering. "Yup, all set."

I stand. "What next?"

"He'll be served, and we go from there."

"And her new address will remain confidential?"

"Yes, victims of abuse can request their address be hidden from their abuser on official documents."

"Okay. Good. Keep me posted."

I turn around to leave when he calls my name. I stop and look at him. "Yeah?"

"I've known you a long time. And I know that look. If you're going to do what I think you're going to do, I'm asking you to reconsider. Let me handle this."

I nod. "Thanks for your help, Justin."

Justin was right. I'm doing exactly what he thinks I'm doing. I'm going to confront Tristan. I'm going to demand that he stay as far away from Zara as possible. I'm also going to tell him that if he doesn't walk away peacefully, not only will I break his neck, but I'll expose him for the piece of shit that he is. It's time. It's been time. I should have never let it get this far. I should have ignored Zara's pleas and protected her a long time ago. Tristan would have never laid a finger on her if I had stepped in. I dropped the ball. I allowed her to get hurt. Now I must fix it. I need her to know without a doubt that she's safe and secure.

This is the only way. Justin said himself that it would be hard to prove what Tristan did to her without evidence or witnesses. The system is fucked up. It's not designed to protect women. A restraining order is nothing more than a piece of paper—it does nothing but demand that a person stay away from another person. It'll do nothing if he decides to find her and try to hurt her. Zara wants freedom. True freedom. And I can't give her that if I'm locking her inside to prevent Tristan from finding her. I can't give her freedom if she's going to constantly look over her shoulder whenever I'm not around. If we have any chance at being happy together, I need to do this. I need to show her that he's no longer a threat to her. That she can move on with her life, with a sense of security she's never felt before. I approach the house with Justin's words yelling in my mind. He told me to let him handle it. As much as I'd like to do that, I can't. I ring the doorbell. The door opens after a few minutes. "What the fuck do you want?"

"I came to talk to you. To offer you a deal."

"A deal? The only deal I'm willing to make is that I won't beat your ass if you tell me where my wife is. I'm sure you know."

I laugh spitefully. "I think you'll want to hear what I have to say. If you want any chance of winning the governor's seat. You are announcing your bid soon, right?"

He frowns. He takes a sip of the clear liquid in his glass and steps to the side. "I'm listening."

I walk inside and immediately notice the stench of alcohol. I follow him into the living room, where he offers me a drink. "Vodka?"

I shake my head. "No."

He walks over to the fireplace and leans against it. "So, let's hear it. What's this deal you want to offer me?"

I stand across from him. "You're going to be served divorce papers. You'll sign them willingly. You'll walk away from the marriage without a peep. You won't ever bother her. You won't ever try to find her. If you happen to see her, you'll act like a stranger to her. I don't even want you *thinking* about her."

He laughs out loud. Vodka-coated spit flying across the room. "Why the fuck would I do something as dumb as that?"

"I have information that could jeopardize your campaign. I have proof of your affair and unborn baby. Proof of your embezzlement and bribes to other politicians. I'm sure they'll want to see you pay for bribing them and would be more than willing to testify against you in court. Do you think the people of Georgia would vote for a cheating, lying person like you?"

"You're lying?"

"Am I? Do you really want to take that chance, Tristan?"

He takes a swig of liquor and places his glass on top of the fireplace mantle. "I need her. I can't run without the image of a supportive wife."

I take a step closer. "You can and you will. Use the sympathy vote. All you need to say is that your marriage failed because you work too much. That you're married to the state of Georgia and that's where your loyalty lies, even at the expense of your marriage."

"You've got this all figured out, huh? You steal my wife, come into my home, and think you can threaten me?"

"The decision is up to you, Tristan. You can take it or leave it."

I have him exactly where I want him. The fear on his face shows me that he knows there's no way out of this unless he does what I'm asking. He could opt not to run for governor, but Tristan is cocky. Selfish. There's no way he would give that opportunity up. He rubs the back of his neck in frustration. "I need another drink. Wait here."

He leaves the room, and I shove my hands inside my pants pocket, glad that he's seeing reason. "Tyson, at least give me time to think about this," he says from behind me.

I turn around to tell him no. That either he agrees to my terms right now, or the deal is off the table and becomes front page news. I turn around to look him in the eyes when I tell him this, but instead of looking him in the eyes, I'm looking down the barrel of a gun. I raise my hands in the air slowly. "Tristan, you don't want to do this. I left specific instructions in case something happens to me."

He shakes his head. "I can't let you ruin this for me, Tyson. It's time to get rid of you."

ZARA

I slept like a baby. It's the most peaceful sleep I've gotten in a long time. I roll over, and my eyes land on the plate of food, placed on a tray beside the bed. I sit up and lift the lid. The sight of pancakes, bacon, and eggs makes my mouth water. Beside it is a note from Tyson telling me he'll be back in a few hours. I smile as I think about him. He asked me to marry him last night. I still can't believe it. Can we really be happy together? Will Tristan really let me go? I don't know the answer to that. All I know is that I'm tired of the abuse. Tired of the mistreatment. I'll never go back to Tristan or that house. I don't care if I need to sue him every month for emotional distress until a judge believes what he did to me. I swing my feet to the side of the bed and notice a new phone on the nightstand. I power it on, and Tyson's number is already programmed. I send him a text.

Me: Thank you for the breakfast. And the new phone. See you when you get home.

Home? I'm jumping to conclusions. Tyson and I didn't discuss where we would live. I love this apartment. It's simple. But I'm sure he won't want to live here. Three apartments could fit into his house. I take a shower and borrow one of his T-shirts. I slide into the jeans I had on yesterday, opting to wear no panties since I don't have any clean ones. I grab the plate of food and carry it in the kitchen to place it inside the microwave. I dial Tyson while I wait for it to heat up. It goes straight to his voicemail. The microwave beeps, and I remove my food and try him again. It goes to his voicemail a second time. I place the phone down on the counter and take a bite of my eggs. I smile as I chew them. I could get used to this, waking up, feeling carefree and happy. Today marks the beginning of a new life for me. A new job, a new home, and a new relationship. The thought of my new position makes me giddy inside. I did it. And not because of how Tyson feels about me. But because of my work. He loved my ideas enough to add them to his collection. And he believed in me enough to let me work with him to get it done. I have so many ideas. So many ways to make his company more profitable, and I can't wait. I'm on cloud nine this morning, but for some reason, I also feel unsettled. This bad feeling has been nagging at me since last night, and I can't seem to figure out what it is. I'm interrupted when my phone rings. It's Tyson. "Hey, you finally called me back."

"Zara. Come home."

"Tristan?"

That nagging feeling settles in my stomach. "If you want to see him alive again, you'll come home."

I'm floored with anger. I'm about to accuse him of lying just to get me back when the phone beeps with an image. It's an image of Tyson lying on the floor. My heart stops beating. "Don't hurt him. I'm on my way."

I can't describe the way I'm feeling right now. It's a mixture of panic, rage, fear, and anxiety. Tyson didn't mention going to see Tristan today, but somehow, I felt it. I felt like something was wrong. I ran out of the house as soon as I ended the call, barely putting on my shoes. I make it to the security station and realize I have no money to call a cab. I pull up my Uber app and order one—the account is linked to Tristan and my bank account, so I know there would be money to cover it. I wait about eight minutes before it shows up. I hop inside, tell the driver it's an emergency, and ask him to hurry. My mind is in a frenzy as we drive, hoping that Tyson isn't hurt.

We arrive at the house, and I jump out of the car, promising to tip him handsomely. I push the door open, but it's locked. I open my purse, hoping I still have my house key when the door swings open. Tristan stands in front of me, covered in blood and holding a gun. He yanks me inside and points the gun at me. "Give me your phone."

I hand it over to him with shaky hands. "What did you do?"

He pushes the gun into my chest. "What did *I* do? This is all your fault, Zar. All of it. Walk."

I walk slowly with my hands raised in the air while he pushes the gun to the middle of my back. "You thought you'd get away from me by fucking Tyson? You two thought you could threaten me and get away with it?"

"Tristan, let's talk about this, please."

"There's nothing to talk about. What you're going to do is call the police. Tell them you and Tyson had an affair and he became upset when you wouldn't leave him. Tell them he showed up here and tried to kill you and we shot him in self-defense."

I pray that Tyson is okay as I enter the living room. I look down and spot him lying on the floor. He doesn't appear to be breathing. I rush to his side, not caring that Tristan's pointing a gun at me. I grab his wrist and feel a faint pulse. I put my ear to his chest and hear faint breathing. I move him. "Tyson, get up."

Tristan paces the floor. "It's no use, Zara. He's gone. And it's all because of you. You almost ruined this for me." He stops, pulls the drapes back, and looks out the window. "Get off the floor. I need you to call the cops and tell them exactly what I told you to."

I don't move. He rushes over and places the gun against the back of my head. "I said get the fuck up, Zara."

I slowly rise to my feet and turn around carefully. "Either

you call the cops and tell them, or I shoot you right here. I'll marry Cicely and won't think twice about what I've done."

"I won't do it. You'll have to kill us both."

"What?"

"You heard me, Tristan. You'll have to kill us both."

He places the gun against my forehead. "You're willing to die for him?"

In all the years I've put up with Tristan's abuse, I could never get to him. No matter what I said. No matter what I did. He was immune to caring. But right now, seeing me willing to die for another man pains him. I can see it in his face. "You don't mean that."

"Yes, I do. Tyson is more of a man than you'll ever be."

His eyes turn hollow. He raises the gun and hits me on the head with it. I fall to the floor, where he kicks me in the face. Flashbacks of the last beating flicker in my head. I made it out last time. This time, I might not be that lucky. When he raises his foot to kick me again, I find the strength to grab it and yank him down. He falls backwards, hitting his head against the coffee table. The gun falls from his hand and tumbles just inches away from me. I dive for it and point it at him. He places his hand at the back of his head as he rises up. "Ahh," he groans. "Zara, put the gun down, baby, please."

"I'm not your baby."

He attempts to get up. "I swear to God if you move one more inch, Tristan, I will shoot you."

I scoot back until I'm next to Tyson. I reach over him and grab his phone that's lying on the floor. Tristan continues to beg me to let him go. "Zara, please."

My fingers shake so badly I accidently drop the gun, and it slides a few inches away from me. Tristan looks down at it then back at me. In a split second, we both dive for it, only I reach it first and pull the trigger. He stumbles back with his hand pressed against his neck. Blood gushes everywhere. He collapses on the floor and doesn't move. I reach for Tyson's phone again, only this time, I hold the gun firmly, just in case he isn't dead. I dial 9-1-1.

"9-1-1, what's your emergency?"

"I need help. I just shot someone."

CHAPTER 17

ZARA

After hours of interrogation, I'm finally released from the police station. I told them everything, starting with the abuse I've been receiving from Tristan. So far, I haven't been charged with killing him, but I've been told not to leave the state and to find a great lawyer, just in case. I don't care if I'm charged. I don't care if they believed me or not. All I care about is Tyson. I kept asking them to get me an update, but they refused. Because I'm technically not family, I don't have the right to any information regarding his medical status. I drove myself crazy with worry, thinking the worst. I can't lose him. He has to be alive. I enter the hospital room. The tears fall as soon as my eyes land on him. He's lying still. With tubes and wires coming from every direction. I rush to his side, pull up a chair, and grab his hand. "Tyson."

He doesn't answer me. "Tyson, please. If you can hear me, squeeze my hand."

Nothing. I place my head on the bed and sob. "Please be okay. I need you."

I'm interrupted by someone clearing their throat. "I'm Dr. Hank."

I stand without letting go of Tyson's hand. "Will he be okay?"

"He's in pretty bad shape. Are you family? I can't discuss his diagnosis unless you are."

"I'm his fiancée."

He looks down at his chart. "Name?"

"Zara Price."

He writes my name down and flips another page. "Mr. Reed sustained life-threatening injuries. It's not looking good."

My heart sinks down to my belly. "Please, there must be something you can do."

Another man walks in. A man I don't know. He looks at Tyson, then at me. "I'm Justin, Tyson's lawyer and executor." He extends his hand and shakes mine. "It's nice to finally meet you, Zara."

I don't know how he knows who I am. Has Tyson spoken about me to him? I would ask, but I honestly don't care right now. Right now, I need to know if they can save him. "Is he going to make it, Doctor?"

He takes a deep breath. "The bullet entered his skull and is lodged in his brain. Unfortunately, it's too risky to operate and remove it."

"So, what does that mean?" Justin asks.

"It means that right now, he's braindead and there's a slim chance of him waking up. If by some chance he does wake up, he'll most likely be in a vegetative state."

I scream out loud and fall to my knees. Justin rushes over to catch me. I sink into his arms sobbing loudly. He pulls me up and steadies me. The doctor gives me a minute before he continues. "We'll need you to decide if you want him to remain on life support."

I shake my head. "No. I can't."

"Doctor, could you give us a few minutes?" Justin asks.

He leaves the room, and Justin turns to me. "Zara, I've known Tyson a very long time. He would not want to live this way."

"No. I can't do it."

"I know this is hard for you. It's hard for me also. Tyson wasn't just a client of mine—he was my friend."

"Then don't say things like that. If he's your friend, help me get him to wake up."

I'm angry. How dare anyone suggest that we just give up and pull the plug? I won't do it. I don't care how long he stays this way. I don't care how much it costs. I'll get five jobs if I have to. "Hey, I'm in this with you. But as his friend, I felt you needed to know what his wishes would be."

"He asked me to marry him. He can't give up."

He smiles. "No. I guess he can't. This may not be a good time, but when the hospital called, I had to rush over and give you these."

"They called you?"

"Yeah, I'm his emergency contact. He wasn't going to remove me until he got married."

He hands me a stack of papers, and I read through them slowly. "What is this?"

"It's his entire life, Zara. His businesses, his stock options, his savings, every asset he owns is yours should he…" He waits a second before finishing his sentence. "Should he be incapacitated or die."

"But he *just* asked me to marry him. Why would he do this so quickly?"

"Because he loves you. It's the first thing he did this morning after you accepted his proposal."

I look up. "You knew he asked me to marry him?"

He nods. "Tyson told me everything."

I rub my temple. "This is a lot to deal with right now."

"I know. But this is important information, and in situations like these, it's my job to make sure that all parties are informed."

"Thank you, Justin. And I'm sorry I yelled at you."

He chuckles. "My wife has a temper. I'm used to it." He looks over at Tyson, and his eyes swell with tears. "I'm going to give you some time alone with him. I'll come back later." He hands me his business card. "If anything changes in the meantime, give me a call."

I place the card in my pocket and sit next to the bed. I grab his hand. "Tyson, I can't let you go." No answer. I rest my head next to his and cry softly.

A few hours later, the doctor walks in with a few nurses and checks his vitals. They speak softly with one another and occasionally glance my way. The nurses leave the room, but the doctor remains. He walks over to me. "Mrs. Price. We'll need to remove the ventilator to see if he can breathe on his own, but it's your decision when. I don't know what the outcome will be, but I brought you some brochures, just in case. It's information about quality of life. I thought it would be helpful."

"How long can he stay in here?"

"We usually give it a few weeks."

I nod. He places his hand on my shoulder. "I'll give you some time."

When he leaves the room, I flip open the brochure. The images are heartbreaking. The patients are all in wheelchairs. They can't talk, they can't feed themselves or use the bathroom. According to the information printed on the brochure, patients like these need around-the-clock care. Justin's words come back to haunt me. Would Tyson really want to live like this? Am I being selfish? This is the hardest decision I've ever had to make. And I'm still not sure if I can make it. The monitor beeps. I place the brochure beside me and grab his hand again. "Tyson, I'm going to let them remove the machine. And I need you to fight, baby. I need you to come back to me."

~

I called Justin and asked him to return to the hospital before they remove the ventilator. He was there within an hour. There's no way I can go through this alone. The doctor and nurses surround the bed. I watch them carefully as they remove the machine responsible for keeping him breathing. When it's all done, he starts breathing on his own after a few tense moments. They take his vitals again. "His vitals are the same. Now, we just wait."

The staff leave the room, and Justin and I remain at Tyson's side, hoping that he continues breathing and that he wakes up. I break the silence. "I should have asked you earlier. Does he have any other family you're aware of?"

"Aunts. Uncles. No one he would consider close enough to call right now."

"Okay."

"He couldn't wait to start a family of his own though."

We didn't have time to get to that part of our relationship. We didn't discuss starting a family or if either of us wanted kids. "How long have you known him?"

"For over ten years."

"That's a long time. Much longer than I've known him."

Justin places his hand inside mine. "Hey, time doesn't matter when it comes to family. Tyson loves you. He trusts you. You're just as important to him as I am."

I smile. "Thank you, Justin."

"I'm glad he has you. The bastard's been looking for love for as long as I've known him."

We both laugh. Trying to lighten the mood a little. "I'll grab a chair and get some work done."

"Okay."

Hours pass, and Tyson is still breathing on his own. The doctors say it's a good sign. I rest my head beside him with his hand in mine as Justin types away on his laptop. I yawn loudly and close my eyes to take a nap. And that's when I feel it. It's faint at first, almost like it never happened. But then it happens again. I lift my head and turn to Justin. "Call the doctor. He just moved."

THREE MONTHS LATER

I kick my heels off as soon as I walk inside my home. Today was a rough one. Meeting after meeting and putting out a few fires. I walk upstairs and enter my bedroom. "How is he today, Margo?"

"Very moody, Mrs. Reed."

I walk over to Tyson, who's facing the television. "Hi, honey," I say slowly.

He looks at me like he wants to say something, but he can't get the words out. He forms his mouth to try and speak again, but he struggles. He becomes frustrated and closes his eyes. The past three months have been an emotional roller coaster. After Tyson woke up that day, he was evaluated for a week before they discharged him. Although he could breathe on his own, his mental capacity was limited. Further tests revealed that only a small percentage of his brain was functional. Justin helped me purchase a home equipped to help me take care of him, and we married a week later. It had been hard convincing the judge that Tyson had the mental capacity to marry, but Justin fought tooth and nail to prove that this was what he wanted. In the end, the judge agreed to honor his wishes. Justin helped me hire the best nursing staff available. They take care of him during the day while I continue to run the company. I know Tyson wouldn't want a company he built from the ground up to collapse. I kneel in front of him. "Let's try again."

He looks into my eyes, and I can see some of the frustration evaporate. I can see the softness appear like he used to look at me. He opens his mouth again. "Woooorrkkk."

He did it. He managed to speak to me. "Work?" I repeat.

"He's been trying to say that word all day, ma'am," Margo adds.

I smile at him. "Work is fine, honey. I'm doing okay."

Guilt slams into my chest, and I kneel before him. This is all my fault. If he hadn't gone to confront Tristan, I would still have him here with me. His life is ruined because of me. I place my hand in his, and he squeezes it lightly. It's our way of communicating. "What is it, sweetheart?"

He tugs my hand faintly. He's not strong enough to grab it, but I can tell that he needs me closer. I place my palm against the side of his face. He moves his face so that his lips brush against my hand. That's it. I know what he wants. A kiss. I lean forward and place my lips on his. He isn't able to kiss me like he used to, but I can feel his attempts to keep them firmly in place. I hold my lips against his for minutes as memories of us flash in my mind. The tears fall and force me to pull my lips away. I stare up at him. "I'm so sorry, baby."

I stand up. "Margo, I'm going to shower. Can you get his dinner ready?"

"Sure, Mrs. Reed."

As soon as I enter the shower, the tears fall. I've been crying every day for the past week. Crying for the wedding we'll never get to have, the honeymoon we'll never get to go on. We'll never be able to have children, live the life we both thought we could have with each other. And it sucks. Every single day I see him this way reminds me of the life that was taken from him. Tyson promised to take care of me. And he kept that promise up until he couldn't. Now, I'm taking care of him. And I promise to do so until the day we die. Brain damaged or not. I love him. And he is who I choose to spend the rest of my life with. I finish my shower, slide into some pajamas, and walk inside my bedroom.

Margo has already set everything up. "Thank you, Margo, I've got it from here."

"Have a good night, Mrs. Reed."

It's been tough juggling my CEO hat and being a wife. I have my hands tied in so many things, but Tyson is my number-one priority. I call home every hour to check on him. I never work late. And once Margo bathes him and places him in bed, I feed him dinner. I climb into bed and position myself next to him. I scoop some mashed sweet potato onto a spoon. "I had to fire someone today, honey."

He opens his mouth, and I slide the spoon inside. "She kept messing up our orders."

He opens his mouth again for more, and I giggle. "You like them, huh? I told Margo to add a little bit of orange juice. Gives it good flavor." I scoop up more and feed it to him. "Anyway, I don't think she respected me anyway. She kept giving me a hard time."

His eyes stay focused on mine, and I know he agrees. "I hired some really talented designers, Tyson."

I attempt to feed him some peas, but he spits them out. I laugh out loud as I wipe his mouth. "I told Margo you wouldn't like these."

I continue to tell him about my day as I feed him, and when I'm finished, we watch a little television before I ask Margo to help me lay him down for the night. I lie beside him, holding his hand while I stare into the shadows. "Tyson, I never got the chance to thank you. Thank you for protecting me. Thank you for saving me." He taps my hand gently. "I should have left him when you told me to. I waited too long. If I had just listened to you, maybe none of this would have happened."

He taps my hand twice this time. "I know what you're saying. It's not my fault."

I place my head on his chest. "I love you."

"I…" he pauses. "Too," he says in a slow drawl.

The next morning, I open my eyes and decide to skip work today. I'd rather stay home and spend some time with Tyson. Maybe I'll take him for a walk. I roll over. He's still asleep, which is unusual. "Tyson, wake up, sweetheart. I'm going to take you to the park today."

He still doesn't open his eyes. "Tyson, wake up, we're going to spend the day together."

I inch closer and grab his hand. "Baby…" He doesn't move. I check his pulse and can barely feel one. I gasp as a tear falls down my cheek. "No," I choke out as my lungs constrict.

"Margo!" I yell. "I need help!"

EPILOGUE

TWO YEARS LATER

TYSON

Well, guys. I know I had you worried there, but I made it. I thought my life was over. I thought I was going to die. Well, technically, I did die for three minutes. And let me tell you what I saw when my heart stopped. I saw my mother. She came to me and told me that what happened to her wasn't my fault. She said that not only did she approve of Zara, but that it was destined for Zara and me to be together. I also saw Zara and me, saying our vows in front of our closest friends and family. I saw her give birth to our first child, then again to our second one. I saw us running through a field of purple lilies with our two small kids running behind us. I saw us growing old together, seeing our kids off to college, becoming grandparents, and then dying at an old age after we've enjoyed a happy life together. It was like the life I could have flashed before my eyes. So, I chose to fight. I fought with everything in me. I've had a long recovery. I was wheelchair bound when I came home from the hospital two years ago. The frustration and helplessness I felt is indescribable. I couldn't do anything by myself. Margo and Zara took turns taking care of me. And when my heart stopped that morning, I heard Zara yelling. I heard her calling for me, telling me she needed me. That she loved me. I followed her voice. I used whatever strength I had to come back to her. And when I did, the road to recovery was brutal. After the doctors got my heart pumping again, I began to start having memories. I began to speak in two to three words. After a year of physical and mental cognitive therapy, I was labeled as a miracle. A person who never should have survived, let alone live a normal life.

"I don't like the green."

I look over at my beautiful wife. She's sitting next to me, wearing my T-shirt, and sketching a new design. Words can't explain how grateful I am to have her. Zara could have taken my money and run. She could have moved on and married someone else, someone she didn't have to care for. But she didn't. She stayed. She took care of me. She loved me. I made a promise to take care of her, and when I couldn't, she in turn took care of me. It made me love her even more. I sneak a peek at her drawing. "I like it."

She giggles. "You say that about everything I design."

I shrug. "Well, what can I say? I'm biased."

She nudges me. "Tyson, come on, this is the ugliest design I've ever sketched."

I shove her notebook off her lap and pull her to me. "Take a break, baby. You've been working non-stop."

She smiles. "As much as I would like to take a break, you know I can't. Not with fashion week around the corner." Her smile disappears. "Did the doctor say if it was okay for you to travel to New York?"

I'm recovered. Back to normal. But I'll always have challenges. I get bad migraines. There are times I feel weak. There are times I become forgetful. If I abide by the doctor's orders, I'm predicted to live a long and happy life. That means no stress and taking it easy. I was instructed not to overexert myself. Zara ran the company when I was incapacitated. I could have gone back once I gained my mental capacity, but I no longer had the desire to return to work. I stepped down and turned it over to her. She's made us richer. She's built a legacy for generations to come. She's done what I knew she was meant to do. She's paved her own way. She's earned her respect. And not because she's the wife of Tyson Reed, but because she's Zara fucking Reed. Fashion mogul and the savviest businesswoman I've ever met. I nod to answer her question. "Yes, I'll be fine to travel, honey."

"Have your headaches come back?"

I kiss her softly on the lips before answering. "No. I've been good."

They've come back full force, and they hurt like a bitch, but I'll never tell her. She worries too much. She studies my face. "Are you sure you're feeling okay?"

I smirk. "I'm sure. Won't you let me show you just how good I'm feeling?"

My hands slide under her shirt, and she stops me. "We just made love two hours ago."

I kiss her neck. "You know I can never get enough of you."

She giggles as my hand slides between her legs. She's about to pull her shirt off when we're interrupted by the sound of crying. She grabs the baby monitor and turns it down. "I'll get her."

Tiana Aliyah Reed. My sweet baby girl. Born two months ago during a thunderstorm, weighing just under six pounds. I spend hours holding her. Making sure she knows her daddy's voice. Letting her feel the security of her father's arms wrapped around her. "No. I've got her. Finish your design, and we'll pick up where we left off later."

I start to slide out of bed, but she grabs my hand, stopping me. She's teary eyed. "I thought I lost you once. Every day, I wake up grateful that we have another chance. I love you so fucking much."

I squeeze her hand. A habit of ours that started two years ago when I could barely speak. "I used to think that success was my destiny, and when I reached it, it wasn't enough. Lying in that hospital made me see that money means nothing, success doesn't mean shit. I didn't care if I couldn't work another day in my life. *You* are what I fought to get back to. You. Us. Tiana. That was my destiny. And guess what, baby. If I had to do it all over again...I would."

THE END

IF YOU OR SOMEONE YOU KNOW IS SUFFERING FROM ABUSE, PLEASE CONTACT THE NATIONAL DOMESTIC VIOLENCE HOTLINE AT

1-800-799-7233

ABOUT THE AUTHOR

L.R. Jackson was born and raised on Maryland's eastern shore. She's a fun and spontaneous Gemini who has an addiction for wings and a passion for food. By day, she works in Corporate America, and by night, she dreams of Alpha Males and Suspenseful Romance.

When she's not playing chauffeur to her teenaged daughter, she can be found reading, cooking, traveling, and of course writing.

She loves to hear from her readers, and you may contact her via:

Facebook: Author L.R. Jackson
Twitter: @AuthorLRJackso1
Instagram: mdgirl1979
Goodreads: L.R. Jackson
www.authorlrjackson.com

ALSO BY L.R. JACKSON